TRUTHTELLING

STORIES
FABLES
GLIMPSES

TRUTHTELLING

Stories

Fables

Glimpses

Lynne Sharon Schwartz

Delphinium Books

TRUTHTELLING

No part of this book may be used or reproduced in any manner
whatsoever without written permission of the
publisher except in the
case of brief quotations embodied in critical articles and reviews.
For information, address DELPHINIUM BOOKS, INC.,
16350 Ventura Boulevard, Suite D
PO Box 803
Encino, CA 91436

Library of Congress Cataloging-in-Publication Data is available
on request.
ISBN 978-1-883285-92-0
20 21 22 LSC 10 9 8 7 6 5 4 3 2 1

First Edition

Artwork and Cover Design by Colin Dockrill, AIGA

Contents

Truthtelling

Back when they were newlyweds, gripped tight by desire, they sometimes played at imagining themselves old. Old but still clear-headed and attractive—at least to each other—seated in adjacent rockers on a porch in some rural setting surrounded by trees, watching the sun slide into a lake. Naturally they had no porch back then, just a three-room apartment in Greenwich Village.

"We'll walk very slowly," she said. "Assuming we can walk."

"Oh, we'll walk all right." Immobility was unacceptable to him. He was big and athletic, soon to become a runner; when it became fashionable he would take it up with zeal, training for marathons that she loyally watched, stopping only in his sixties when a knee injury proved intractable.

"We'll swim in the lake. Maybe we'll have kayaks. We can call across the water."

"We might need hearing aids," he said.

"We'll communicate by telepathy. Then we can tell each other the truth," she said, reaching for the last slice of pizza. "Sure you don't want this?" She held it up in both hands like an offering. It was a hot August evening; after work she'd changed into skimpy shorts and a tank top. Offering the pizza was like offering herself.

He studied her legs attentively, folded in a near lotus

position: she was an early yoga devotee, before everyone took it up. "No, go on, take it. As far as truth, I'd rather hear it out loud. But anyway we'll have told the truth all along, won't we?" He was a lawyer, familiar with how slippery a package the truth was. At thirty, a newly made partner in a major firm. Soon they would be moving to a larger apartment.

"We don't know what's waiting for us in the future. There might be some little lies along the way. Nothing serious." She was a more languid sort, with a body verging on lush. An art lover, with a slight talent for drawing, she stayed sleek for her job in a Chelsea gallery; she was new enough there to feel her heart leap when well-known painters dropped in. At home she took up weaving, a sedentary pastime. Her loom stood steadfastly in the various bedrooms in the various apartments they would share, even when she gave it up after a few years. There were the children to see to.

They met at a mutual friend's party and were drawn to each other instantly: a series of glances, growing less tentative, till at last, an approach. His. The more romantic, he later claimed it was love at first sight but she didn't believe in such things. Lust at first sight is more like it, she said. She pretended it took her a few weeks to be captivated—captured—but he suspected she was lying. Some kind of misplaced pride, most likely. One of the little lies, from the start.

"But why just then, if we've kept secrets all along?" he asked.

"Because then it'll be too late."

"For what?"

"Oh, you know, divorce. Bitterness. Distrust. All of that. We'll keep that out of the picture."

"That goes without saying," he said. "But chances are we'll be talking about the grandchildren while we sip gin-and-tonics and rock in our chairs. One a rocket scientist, one a rock star."

"What if there aren't any?"

"We'll adopt. Can you adopt grandchildren?"

She tossed the pizza crust into the cardboard box and leaned towards him. "Shall we go into the bedroom and lie down for a while?"

There was no need to adopt. None of the grandchildren were rock stars or rocket scientists but they were perfectly gratifying, indeed perfect. And now, in the anticipated future, they had the porch, with comfortable chairs, though no rockers—too suggestive of resignation. It was a summer house in a woodsy area on the anticipated lake, an hour's drive from the city. They found, as they aged, that they couldn't give up the city. The family was there, the friends, the movies and cafés, the local routines—the chirpy woman in the fruit market, the silent man at the dry cleaners, the Pakistani who ran the newsstand. The dog walker with African braids who managed six at a time.

Since his retirement from the law firm, he volunteered for good causes. Big Brother to a ghetto kid. Adviser to younger professionals. Basketball coach at the community center. Plus some gardening at the weekend house—vegetables, pungent herbs, glossy eggplants. She learned to throw pots and babysat for the grandchildren and enrolled in courses around the city: economics (she'd always wanted to understand that), the history of Near Eastern art, computer science, at which she proved unexpectedly adept. She fooled around with inventing a video game; maybe one day she'd finish it. They were members of a certain class and generation, and felt faintly guilty about their stereotypical customs, their privileges. But they were unique among their acquaintances in one way: they had never divorced. Envious friends asked how they'd kept going for so long. They'd look at each other, smile diffidently, and shrug.

They could still manage the drive to the house most weekends, taking turns back and forth, aware that there soon might come a time when they couldn't. There would come a time . . . A shared knowledge, unspoken. Not today or even tomorrow, but inevitable. It was happening all around them, a blight: their weeks were punctuated by visits to the sick and, worse, memorial services. There was a sense of valiantly doing their best, while knowing their turn would come.

Again it was a warm late summer evening. They sat on the porch drinking iced tea, watching the changing patches of glimmer on the lake. The evening gin-and-tonics they'd looked forward to gave them headaches the next morning.

"Maybe it's time for the conversation," she said.

"What conversation?" He was enjoying his daily cigarette and didn't relish being distracted. Each precious inhalation had to be savored.

"You know. Don't play dumb."

"Must we? I thought it was only a game."

"What about that secretary in the office, the one with the high heels and short skirts?"

"There were so many like that. Which do you mean?"

"You know the one I mean. Shall I pour you some more?" She lifted the pitcher of iced tea.

"Just a little, thanks." He paused to hold up his glass. "Okay. But I barely remember it. It was only a couple of months." A little lie. He remembered quite well the elation of beginning, the pain of ending, and everything in between.

She gave a self-satisfied nod. "I knew it! I'm never wrong about those things. Remember when I told you Thea and Hank would split up? I knew even before they did. Did you suffer?"

"Some."

After a while, she said, "Don't you want to tell me anything about it?"

"Not especially."

"Or ask me anything?"

"No. Only if you're eager to confess . . ."

"It's not confession. Simply truth. Then we can die with everything clear between us."

"Who said anything about dying? And nothing's ever totally clear, not even in the courtroom. But go ahead. I can see you want to."

"When Abby was about a year, I . . . I had an abortion."

He jerked quickly forward and his glass tipped, spilling some of the tea, but, ever the athlete, he caught it before it could fall to the floor. "What! I never knew. You did it without telling me?"

"I know." She hung her head. "That was a neat catch. Anyway, yes, that was bad, I mean not telling you. But I wasn't sure . . . you know? I didn't want to risk it."

"You weren't sure . . . You mean . . .? Whose did you think it could be?"

She stared at the lake for a moment before she answered. "Larry Brooks. But to tell the truth, I just didn't know."

"That creep? How could you?"

"You're right. It was a big mistake. Much regret."

She seemed eerily calm about the whole business. He had to assume Larry Brooks had qualities he couldn't appreciate. He lit another cigarette.

"That's your second."

"Thanks for noticing. I'm aware of that."

"Oh, come on, we're too far along for sulking."

"But I had no idea . . . How long did it last?"

"On and off, oh, I don't remember, a year, year and a half? It was when you were out of town a lot on that orphanage case."

"I would have thought you had better taste." He suddenly sat upright. It was no longer a game. "The kids? Are you sure? If you tell me that—"

"Take it easy. Of course I'm sure. What do you take me for?"

"I don't know anymore what to take you for."

She smiled. "Take me as you always have. Nothing's changed. Now your turn."

He didn't like the idea of turns. He might not be able to keep up with her. Or the opposite—he might have to keep going long after she'd finished. Which of them had the most to tell? He'd always considered her the more open of the two, but now he wasn't sure. "I cheated at squash once when I was playing with Bill Ross. But long ago."

She laughed. "That's not too awful. Why'd you do it?"

"I was waiting to be made partner. Getting impatient."

"Wouldn't it have been better to let him win?"

"No. He respects winners. I was made partner a few weeks later."

"Did you ever steal any money, I mean big money?"

"No! How could you even think that? I'd never do that. All I ever did was pad the bills now and then, like everyone else. Only with clients who wouldn't feel the difference. We had our sense of honor, after all." He smiled at his own wit.

"Any other of the girls in the office?"

"Certainly not." The very idea. What did she take him for? "Are we done now?"

"I wrote most of Diana's essays on her college applications. Rewrote, I mean. She didn't have the patience and I wanted her to get in, you know."

"That hardly counts. I'm sure you're not the only one. And she did get in."

"Yes. But I felt guilty."

More guilty, he noted, than she felt about Larry Brooks and the abortion.

"Well . . . ," she said.

More? He took a breath, wondering at this sudden craving for revelation. He didn't share it at all.

"Well, there was this woman at the gym I got friendly with, you know, locker-room chatter, and then I realized she was interested in me, I mean, coming on to me. We had coffee a couple of times. For a little while I considered it, just for . . . I don't know . . . curiosity. But I never did. I didn't really want to."

"Oh, am I supposed to be flattered?"

"That's up to you. I'm just reporting. What about falling in love?"

Years back when they imagined this conversation, she'd said there would be no danger, so late in the game. But he sensed danger in the darkening air. Still, he felt an obligation to play, at least to make a respectable showing. "There was something, once. But I averted it. A client. I didn't . . . I dreaded where it might lead. But it was very tempting. I passed the case on to someone else."

"Was it that condo case in Midtown? You said you gave it up because of some conflict of interest."

"I'm impressed that you remember."

"Do you want to tell me about her?"

"It was so long ago . . ." In truth he'd buried it so deep it would take too much effort to disinter. What he remembered was the feeling, the heat that came over him when she entered his office, the flush and itch of starting something new. She was nothing at all like his wife, his true love, he remembered that well. He was not a man with a "type," like the men he knew who divorced and promptly found a new woman who looked and sounded just like the discarded wife.

No, best to let that story lie. "And you?" he asked, aiming at a tone of mild curiosity. "Love?"

"Love? No, I've said all there is. Give me one of those, would you?"

He handed her the cigarettes and lighter. How to know if she was telling the truth? Her revelations, however startling, had been so few. "Are you playing by the rules?"

"Absolutely," and she inhaled with a pleasure that was close to erotic.

"In that case I'm done too."

"Really? I expected more of you." She held up the cigarette and looked at it. "This is making me dizzy after so many years without. But it's a nice feeling. Why not go back to bad habits, at this point?"

"That time we quit together," he said, "I used to smoke in the office. That was when you still could. I didn't want you to think I had no willpower."

She waved her hand dismissively, as if this peccadillo were too minute to consider. "What does it matter now? We've said enough, haven't we?" She looked over at him with an inscrutable expression. Wry, affectionate, a hint of mystery. The kind of look that suggested imminent sex years ago, and still did.

"Enough for what?" he asked.

"Just enough. For now."

"For good. I'm not doing it again. Do you think this

was a good idea?" he persisted.

"I think so. It sort of . . . puts things in perspective, doesn't it?" She reached her hand across the distance between their two chairs. "Everything okay?"

He reached out and took her hand, squeezed it hard. The last tiny segment of sun was disappearing into the lake. "Okay then," he said. "The bugs are coming out. Shall we go in and maybe lie down for a while?"

That same indulgent, assenting look. "Why not?"

I Want My Car

I am at this point more than a little concerned about my car, a 2018 red Acura that I keep in excellent condition. It is over two weeks since my ex-wife, Mona (well, not yet officially ex-), called and asked to borrow the car to visit her mother, who was yet again having some sort of health crisis; she lives in an assisted care facility a couple of hours out of the city. There are long-distance buses that stop very near the facility, which during the five years of our marriage Mona used often, except on the occasions when I went with her and drove—infrequent, I admit. But I thought rather than mention the buses, which might lead to an argument about my selfishness and other traits Mona likes to point out, I'd lend her the car. I could afford to be generous and anyway I didn't need it that day, a Saturday. We agreed she would park it on my street when she returned in the late afternoon. I told her where it was parked and said she should get the keys from my doorman and leave them with him later, since I was planning to be out most of the day. I offered my best wishes to her mother, which Mona did not take graciously, but aside from that the transaction went smoothly.

I did almost all the driving during our marriage. Mona is not a particularly good driver, in fact she has disliked driving ever since she was in an accident shortly before we met. She hit a car while merging on the Taconic Parkway, granted, a perilous road, and suffered injuries to her neck, which have bothered her on and off ever since, despite her visits to chiropractors and acupuncturists. Fortunately the other driver was unhurt. The Taconic is the best route to her mother's place. Naturally I didn't bring this matter up by saying, Be careful, or anything of the kind, which I thought showed admirable restraint on my part.

I spent the day biking and picnicking in the park with Susan, whom I recently met through an online dating site, and when we returned at around six, planning to order a pizza and watch a movie, I didn't see the car on the street. Fred, the doorman, said Mona had not come by with the keys.

I phoned her immediately. I had no special need for the car the next day, Sunday, but I was worried and wanted to make sure she was all right.

She was fine, she said. She'd been too tired to bring the car back, then take a bus or cab to her apartment across town. It was safely parked on her block and she would return it the next day.

It was a relief to learn that both she and the car were unhurt. "Fine," I replied. "How is your mother?"

"Doing better. We sat out on the lawn. It was a lovely day. As you surely know."

"Yes. Well, good. I'm glad to hear it. So, just leave the keys with Fred. Make sure you park on the side where it's legal for Monday since I may not be using it until Tuesday or Wednesday."

She agreed. I wish I could say I had a pleasant evening with Susan, but there was some silly fuss about the choice of movie—she found everything I suggested too violent, and this escalated into an unnerving discussion of men's and women's preferences in movies, as these things can do. It ended with her walking out in a huff, leaving me to clean up the pizza crusts, which in their unsightly disarray seemed a symbol of our brief and now messy affair.

I looked for the car on Sunday but didn't find it.

Mona didn't answer when I called so I waited until Monday evening to leave another message; I know from experience that she doesn't like to be disturbed at work. I might have sounded a trifle curt, but I'd been looking forward to having the car back safe and sound, parked where I could see it from my window.

She didn't call back, which was not surprising; Mona has always been careless about returning calls, as well as many other things. I called Tuesday evening but again she didn't pick up. I was almost sure she was home because her book group meets at her place the second Tuesday of the month. I hoped she'd return the call after they left, but no luck.

On Wednesday I really needed the car for a trip to Queens to get a deposition from a client who was housebound. I called Mona at eight in the morning. She answered sleepily.

"Oh, the car. I'm so sorry, really. I just forgot. I'll bring it back tonight."

"But I need it today. I have to go to Queens."

"Take the 7 train from Times Square. It's very quick. I used to do it all the time when I was teaching at that high school."

I remembered that phase well. She complained ceaselessly about the subway trip and I suspect she would have liked to use the car, but I needed to have it available in case something came up. I was reluctant to let Mona use the car for the reasons I've stated. I do feel possessive about the car, as she often reminded me during our marriage. I'd worked hard for it and chosen it carefully. I guess you could say I loved the car almost as if it were a pet. Throughout our marriage I'd wanted a dog, but Mona objected; she didn't much like dogs (she was bitten on the leg once as a child and never quite got over the experience) and claimed she'd be the one who wound up walking it most of the time, which was probably true. Anyway, she didn't last long at that teaching job in Queens. She found the kids unruly and disrespectful; Mona is easily rattled. She left and got a job at a magazine as a graphic designer, where she was still working when we parted three months ago.

When I left, I should say. Leaving was my idea. It caused awful scenes that still send the adrenalin zipping through me when I think of them, which I try not to do. In spite of her many criticisms of me, Mona wanted us to remain together. She said we could work things out if we sat down and talked frankly, or even went to couples therapy, which did not appeal to me; I was sure I'd find it tedious. I have very little tolerance for boredom. Frankly, I was bored with Mona. I never said this outright, I didn't want to hurt her more than necessary. Some people might think this an insufficient reason to leave. A couples therapist might well take that view, or try to talk me out of my boredom. In any case, I didn't relish sitting with a stranger and listening to Mona's complaints about me, or, on my part, listing the many things about Mona that I had come to find wearisome. As I said, that would be hurtful, and I couldn't think of any other valid reasons I could give for wanting to be free of her. Perhaps I'm just not cut out for a long relationship. We were madly in love when we married. I was drawn by what I then saw as her joie de vivre, a quality I'm aware that I lack. But my fascination quickly palled as joie de vivre revealed itself as flightiness and impulsiveness that made her very hard to deal with.

I hadn't been unfaithful, as she accused. I simply wanted to be on my own, without having to consider another person's taste in food and entertainment and politics and friends and all the rest. By the end we disagreed about everything, including where we should live, how we should spend vacations . . . The only things we didn't argue about were money and sex, which I've read are the two matters that bring most marriages to an end. Sex with Mona started out fine, but grew more and more infrequent the more we quarreled about everything else. I didn't want any more nights of her turning her back and curling towards her edge of the bed.

It's true we disagreed about the car. Mona resented the fact that I chose it without consulting her, although she rarely drove and never once expressed a desire for a car. I came home one night and told her I'd gotten myself a birthday present. I wanted something special, and all Mona had gotten me—gotten us, I should say—were two tickets to a popular Broadway show I had no interest in seeing but which she had been talking about for weeks.

"A birthday present?" she said in surprise. "What? What could you possibly need? You're the man who has everything."

This wasn't precisely true, but I did indulge myself in clothes, wines, books, and whatever else I liked. Why not? I made enough money, much more than Mona did, but I never alluded to that fact. I would have been glad to see Mona spend more liberally on herself. Frugality is not one of my faults, which Mona herself would attest to. But she has very simple tastes and needs. She mostly wore jeans and shirts even when she was teaching, and I must confess her lack of interest in clothes sometimes embarrassed me, for instance when we went out to dinner with my colleagues. I bought her expensive dresses, in the hope that she would wear them on such occasions. She thanked me halfheartedly. She'd put them on if I urged her, but she never chose them on her own.

Anyhow, the car. I took the subway to Queens for my meeting and understood why she used to complain about the trip. I got a cab back. I was irritated about the car but determined to restrain myself. It was only a matter of another day or two.

Then something occurred to me. Maybe there'd been some kind of accident on the Taconic that she was keeping from me. Obviously Mona was fine—she sounded fine, that is—but what if the car had been totaled? A wave of nausea swept through me as I imagined my beautiful car bruised and battered, hoisted up in some garage, all its nether parts exposed, while incompetent mechanics fussed over it. Or dead entirely, in a junk heap.

I called Mona late Wednesday night. "Please tell me," I said. "Is the car okay? Did anything happen to it? I'm getting worried."

She laughed. "I know you love that car, Ed. I was very careful with it, believe me. If the car and I were both wrecked you'd shed more tears for it than for me."

"That's not true at all. But I'm speaking to you, I assume you're all right. I really don't know about the car since I haven't seen it."

"The car is fine. I just haven't had time to get it over to you."

"What are you so busy with? Why can't you just drive it over after work? If you want, I'll gladly pay for your cab home."

"That won't be necessary. I'll bring it over this weekend, promise."

"You're sure you're not playing with me? I'll believe that car is okay when I see it."

"You'll see it soon. Over the weekend."

I was getting furious. "Why the weekend? It's Wednesday."

"If I have time I'll do it sooner. Otherwise, the weekend."

"This is outrageous, Mona."

"You never let me drive that car the whole time you had it. That was outrageous. Now you can live without it for a few more days."

"Mona, you never liked to drive."

"That's irrelevant. It was your birthday present to yourself. You wouldn't lend it to anyone, like a little kid."

I sighed. "Okay, let's not get into an argument. Please return the car as soon as you can. I need it for work."

"Understood."

"How are you getting on, by the way?" I asked.

"Fine," Mona said. "Good night."

This conversation left me shaken. I had no choice but to believe that the car was all right. I could do nothing but wait until she made up her mind to stop this rigmarole. It occurred to me that I could call the police, but I didn't want to go that far. Knowing Mona, I was sure it would just make things worse. If only I had a spare set of keys I could go to her neighborhood and search for the car, but I forgot the extra set when I left, along with a few other items of value which I'd like to get back when things between us calm down.

That phone call was over a week ago. I won't go into the inconveniences I've suffered since then, except to say I've taken a lot of taxis. When the weekend passed and there was no sign of the car, I frankly wasn't surprised. I called her once and left a message. In return I got an email that read, "Ed, your car has left you just as you left me. Now you know what it feels like."

That was absurd. And typical of Mona's thinking. The car didn't leave of its own volition, for one thing. I loaned it to her. And I know that someday it will return, while I won't. If there was any remote chance of my returning, it's been dashed by this latest episode.

From the crazy reasoning in her message, I came to understand that Mona has no intention of returning the car anytime soon. She may do so after a while, when I've stopped calling her about it, or when she gets tired of moving it from one side of the street to the other every couple of days, or when her anger at me dissipates, whenever that might be. I still don't want to bring the police into this. I have no wish to be punitive—I just want my car. Eventually I'll have it, I suppose, but I hate to think of the aggravation I'll have to go through to get it.

It's also occurred to me that I could simply buy a new car and chalk this one up to the collateral damage of our separation. It's not out of the question. I was awfully fond of it, but I could probably find one just like it. By the same token, Mona can, and probably will, get a new husband, but not, I imagine, one just like me.

A Lapse of Memory

I was horrified to realize I'd forgotten about my mother. I don't mean I left her waiting impatiently on some street corner, nothing like that. I mean I had forgotten her altogether, forgotten her existence. Or rather it was as if she had died, and died long enough ago that I no longer thought of her frequently. It's shocking that I can even articulate these words, but I insist on facing up to the truth—the appalling deeds, or omissions, one is capable of. I hadn't thought of my mother in weeks, though normally I telephone every few days to see how she is, and every couple of weeks I drive up to see her in the suburban gated community where she lives with her younger sister.

Her sister never married and has taken on the responsibility of caring for my mother—a task she seems to enjoy; she likes the company, and my mother can be pleasant enough when she makes an effort. She is not sick but is growing frail and has difficulty walking, complains constantly of the arthritis in her knees. Nor is she a presence one can easily ignore. My aunt, the caretaker, or caregiver I should say, works part-time in the linen section of a nearby department store. But her schedule is flexible and my mother can be left alone for several hours a day. (She wears one of those gadgets around her neck that you can press for help in case of an emergency, a fall, or any mishap, but so far she has never used it.) I must say I don't know what she does during those solitary hours. There's always television, but since she doesn't see too well at this point, I'm not sure how useful television can be. She has a few remaining friends she may talk to on the phone. Maybe she listens to music. She's always been a music lover and was a wonderful singer in years past.

Anyway, I am straying from the point, which is that I simply forgot about her existence, forgot to call or visit as I regularly do. She could have called me, I thought with a pang; maybe she could ask how I'm doing, for a change. But that doesn't excuse my lapse. I wasn't even extremely busy at work, which might have made me forgetful. I'm on the staff of a small nonprofit for disabled children, and unfortunately we're never very busy. Our cause doesn't have the urgent appeal of environmental issues or political campaigns. I'm fairly sure nothing too bad happened to my mother during my lapse of memory: my aunt would have let me know. But that doesn't excuse my forgetting.

I am aware that people forget things more often as they age, but I'm not yet at that forgetful age, and besides, what people forget are things like where they left their keys or where they parked their cars, not their mothers. I've never heard of anyone forgetting a mother. I've heard people say they've lost their mothers, which is a euphemistic way of saying they died, but my mother was not lost in either sense, dead or missing. Simply forgotten. I know others who lose touch with their mothers because of some bitter rift, or some ancient wrong that allegedly marred their lives, but that's not the case with me and my mother. Indeed, I love my mother, not a consuming love such as some people feel for their mothers, but sufficiently. I have no simmering resentment for anything she did that marred my life; I take personal responsibility for any marring that may have taken place. She was—is—a fairly good mother, as mothers go: at this point in our lives I don't expect a great deal of mothering (though she could call occasionally to see how I am). Whatever her flaws, she certainly does not deserve to be wiped out of my memory. Well, not totally wiped out; I did remember yesterday, during dinner with a man I've dated a few times. But wiped out for a period of several weeks, I'm not sure how many.

What finally brought her to mind was that the man I was having dinner with ordered lemon meringue pie for dessert, something that does not often appear on menus lately, I don't know why. Perhaps it's too humble or old-fashioned, and it's difficult to make well. My mother used to make the most spectacular lemon meringue pie; the meringue part was always perfect, whipped and airy and light, with just a touch of brown on the tips of the swirls. Personally I preferred the lemon part. In any event, when I saw the pie placed in front of my date I suddenly remembered my mother, the continuing existence of my mother, and I must have had a startled look on my face because the man asked what was the matter. I told him about my mother's pies and how I had lately forgotten her, which couldn't have made a very good impression but just then I really didn't care. Had I been alone I would have called her immediately. But I didn't want to talk to her in front of an almost stranger, especially as I'd have to apologize for not having called in so long and it might be a long conversation while she filled me in on the last few weeks—not that her life is burdened with activities, but she tends to run on and I'm generally content to listen. I like the sound of her voice, soft and low, what Shakespeare says is an excellent thing in woman. Also I find it rude when people make or receive phone calls in restaurants and ignore the person they're with.

The man seemed sympathetic and offered me a bite of his pie. It was good, but nowhere near as good as my mother's. I made a note to tell her this when I called later, or tomorrow: that I'd tasted a piece of lemon meringue pie in a restaurant and it was not nearly as good as hers.

I planned to call my mother as soon as I got home. My relationship with the man was possibly at the point where I might have invited him up to my apartment, but this business with my mother had so upset me that I simply got out of the taxi and said good night. I hoped he'd call again, but my investment of feeling was not yet such that I would suffer if he didn't. When I got inside I realized it was too late to call. Not very late, only a little past ten, but I remembered from my childhood how she got alarmed when the phone rang after nine-thirty or ten; anyone calling at that hour, she felt, could only be bringing bad news. I didn't want to alarm her. I'd waited this long, I could wait until tomorrow.

The next day was Saturday. I got up late and dithered around the apartment for a while, putting off calling my mother. I'd have to invent some reason for my failure to keep in touch, though I hate lying, especially to people I care about. My job wasn't the sort that required unexpected business trips. I could say I'd been sick, but that would alarm my mother and was, besides, a cheap excuse. Anyway, she'd see through any excuse I gave; my mother was like that—uncanny at seeing through me. That had been the cause of some skirmishes between us when I was a teenager; she always knew if I'd smoked pot or slept with some boy or had a few drinks. To avoid lying I would keep silent, but she could see behind my silence, and I resented that power more than I resented her scoldings. Still, I couldn't possibly tell the truth, that I had forgotten her existence. I hoped she wouldn't intuit it.

Finally I called, hoping I'd get my sweet-natured aunt, who would be pleased to hear from me and would say, "How are you? We haven't heard from you in a while," but not in a guilt-inducing way. My mother answered the phone. Hearing her soft, low voice was a bit startling, as if in some part of my mind I still believed she no longer existed.

"Hi, Mom. It's me. How've you been?"

She was fine, except for her arthritic knees. She told me about a movie she'd seen with my aunt—somehow her knees carried her there—and a good meal she'd had in a Middle Eastern restaurant down the block. She didn't ask how I was, which wasn't unusual, and she didn't seem bothered by my recent silence.

"I'm sorry I haven't called in a while," I said. "I got busy at work, and then a good friend of mine is going through a divorce and I had to hold her hand. But I've been thinking of you." Lies, all lies, just what I wanted to avoid. But they came out of my mouth nonetheless.

"That's okay. To tell the truth, I didn't notice," she said. "I must have lost track of time. Now that I think of it, yes, it's been a while."

Not at all what I expected.

Instead of feeling relief, like I'd gotten away with something, I was disappointed. I wanted to get off the phone as soon as I could, to think over what this meant. The rest of the conversation was unremarkable. I forgot to tell her about the restaurant's lemon meringue pie that hadn't been as good as hers, a fact I had saved up to please her. Possibly I'd thought it would mitigate my long silence. But my silence needed no mitigating. She hadn't noticed it. I told her I'd see her next weekend, and we said goodbye.

Upon reflection, it was only too clear that my mother had suffered the same memory lapse as I had. She'd forgotten my existence. Even though unlike me she was at an age when forgetfulness is to be expected, she wasn't, as far as I could tell, suffering from any mental impairment. Her chatter had been quite coherent, with any number of small details from the past weeks. She had simply forgotten me. It was unforgivable. Naturally she wouldn't say so, any more than I would say so to her.

Or maybe it was worse. Maybe she didn't ever recall my existence between my routine calls and visits. If that were so, and more and more I was coming to believe it was, then her defection was more extreme, more shocking, than my own.

To forget a mother is bad, granted, but not entirely beyond imagining; after all, one day my mother would be gone, and there might well come a time when I didn't recall her for weeks on end. But to forget a child . . . No, that was unthinkable. My mother had done the unthinkable. Perhaps I would never call her again. But that would be a pointless revenge. She wouldn't notice.

The Golden Rule

It started innocently enough. Could Amanda pick up a few groceries—it was raining so hard. Mail a letter (addressed in such light pencil that Amanda doubted it would ever arrive)? Program Maria's new alarm clock—digital, baffling—for the hours of her medications? Amanda thought nothing of it. It was the sort of thing you do for a frail old neighbor. They lived on the same floor of a solid downtown building where Maria, it seemed, had occupied her apartment since the dawn of time. The other neighbors were newer, young families, everyone running off to work and school, the building left to nannies and maids. How could she refuse?

Over the last month or two, though, the phone calls had become more frequent, their tone more pressing. Would Amanda fetch a prescription at the drugstore, have something copied at the local shop? In mid-October, Maria opened her door as Amanda was coming in—she'd taken a rare half day off to do some shopping—and handed her a set of keys to her apartment. Just in case, she said, her voice obsequious, petulant. "And do you have a minute to come in and call the doctor for me? I can't cope with his new phone system, pressing all those buttons and in the end you don't even get a real person."

"Sure. I'll just get rid of these packages and be right back."

*   *   *

When Amanda and Jack moved in twenty years ago, Maria had been the age Amanda was now, and quite able to manage her own errands as well as attend the nearby church most mornings. Even then she was tiny, bird-like, a bird without feathers or song, who spoke in whispers as if she feared eavesdroppers. She had an unlisted phone number, she'd told Amanda, in a tone that suggested lurking menace. She always wore a navy-blue kerchief tied under her chin—Amanda would rather have died than be seen in such a thing—and white Peter Pan–collared blouses, dark skirts and stockings, Oxford shoes. Slacks, never, even in the coldest weather. Over the years her costume had remained the same but her voice had grown weaker, though no less tinged with complaint.

Amanda had never been in Maria's apartment before. Its gloom was startling: moss-colored drapes on the windows, massive dark furniture, and a stale, sequestered smell, reminding her of grottos she'd visited in Italy long ago. Bits of paper littered the dining room table, jotted notes in a prim, upright handwriting, like a convent schoolgirl's. The doctor's phone number, when Maria finally located the scrap of paper, was written in that maddening number 4 pencil, so faint that Amanda had to read it under one of the fringed lamps.

Returning home was like coming out of an afternoon movie to the stun of brightness. Amanda's own apartment was splashed with color, open to the light. After Jack's death five years ago she had immersed herself in redecorating projects. She'd also made sure to keep her clothes in order, get her hair cut regularly, not let things go. It had been disheartening, at first, to look at her face in the mirror: it wasn't so much the minuscule lines or the no-longer-glow-ing skin—she was familiar with the concoctions to remedy those. It was the somber resignation in the eyes, the slack-ening of the profile, the downward slant of the mouth that suggested disappointment and an unappealing severity. She felt herself in a permanent battle with time and nature, and though in the end she would lose, as everyone does, she re-solved to fight valiantly to the death. She had the means and the will.

Several weeks later Maria called at six in the morning to say she had terrible pains in her stomach.

Ben, who'd slept over because of a thunderstorm, rolled over and grunted irritably, so Amanda took the phone into the living room. "Did you call the doctor?"

"It's too early. They're not in yet. Anyway, he's out of town and I don't like the substitutes."

"But even so . . . Do you want me to call?"

"No, I told you." Maria's voice was becoming a whim-per. "I didn't get any sleep all night, the pain was so bad."

The emergency room, Amanda declared. She'd get dressed and take her.

"No, no emergency room. They make you wait for hours, and you have to sit with all kinds of people."

"I'll call an ambulance, then. They'll take you right away." This she knew from Jack's heart attack. Arrive in an ambulance and you get first-class treatment.

No, those doctors were just students. She didn't trust them. And no, she didn't want Amanda to come over.

"Well, I don't know what else I can do." She struggled to keep her voice even, her impatience in check. "I'll phone you later from work. If it gets any worse, call 911."

"Her again?" Ben muttered, throwing an arm over

Amanda. And after she explained, "So if she won't let you help, then why'd she call?"

"Not to be alone with it, I guess." She knew what that felt like. She'd often been tempted to call friends at the slightest change in Jack's condition, simply not to bear the information alone, as if she were in a narrow space with a large package and needed help carrying it—not that it was so heavy, only very hard to maneuver. She'd given in to the urge, though it hadn't helped much. Her daughter, Jessica, had phoned daily—she was in Spain then, with a new baby. She'd flown back in time for the funeral.

"Tell her you can't be her personal assistant—you have a business to run." He couldn't see why Amanda capitulated: she should do what was convenient and refuse the rest. Ben, a vigorous sixty-eight, was ten years older than Amanda and prided himself on not being "needy"—he liked to show he was up on current buzzwords. Of course he wasn't needy, Amanda thought: he had a housekeeper and a secretary. But she knew better than to say that. He was easy and compliant. Best of all, he was firmly settled in his own place uptown and busy with his accounting practice, leaving her free to spend long hours at the shop. Jack, whom she had loved to distraction, hadn't been easy in any way, especially near the end. But he'd never talked smugly about neediness. He would have understood why she gave in to Maria, would even have been amused. Always into self-improvement, he used to tease. Is that so bad? she asked. Not bad, he said, just a whole lot of work. He would have understood Maria's strategy too: the cunning tyranny of the weak. And grasped that in Amanda, so clearly strong—large, firm-voiced, competent, occupying space with the authority of ownership— Maria had found the perfect foil.

"She probably just has gas pains," Ben said, and rolled

over. Was that what he'd say if she woke up one morning in agony? Kindness, Amanda thought, but didn't care to explain to him at six-fifteen in the morning, shouldn't depend on convenience, or even affection. If it did, it couldn't be called kindness. She was following the Golden Rule, after all, doing unto others . . .

Did Maria follow the Golden Rule? Not very likely. She was mean-spirited, bigoted. She whispered carping comments about the neighbors, and the things she said about their West Indian cleaning women made Amanda shudder. Everything about her was scant and pinched, plus she hardly ate—a refusal of life that irked Amanda—and her clothes were dreadful, though this, Amanda knew, was hardly relevant; she noted it in her inventory only because she thought about clothes all the time—she owned a selective upscale boutique and chose every item herself.

Of course, none of this should matter. Charity need not be deserved, nor should it be offered grudgingly, in bad faith. Her objections, Amanda knew, were more than uncharitable. They were suspect, rising as they did from the pit of her own dread.

She couldn't sleep any more—the call had left her jittery. She moved closer to Ben and asked, "Do you still think I'm beautiful? Or am I becoming an old lady?"

"Of course you're beautiful. Why do you even ask?"

"It's good to hear it once in a while."

"You're beautiful. This part is beautiful, and this, and this." At first he sounded tired, mechanical, but as he went on, his voice gathered enthusiasm. He moved his hands down her body, enumerating, making it a game. "I can't get anywhere below the knee from this position, and I'm too comfortable to move."

"Never mind. That's enough."

"You know what's especially beautiful?"

"What?"

"Here. The hipbone. I like the way it pokes out."

"Don't talk about bones, please."

"Well, I like what's around them. Your wrists are very nice too. And your hands. The fingers are really long. Look, I'll show you what they can do."

Was this, what he wanted of her now, also a species of kindness? She had brought it on herself, asking if she was beautiful. She'd never asked before and now wished she hadn't; beautiful or not, she was tired.

Afterwards, she lay in his arms and ran through the teenagers in the building, the ones Maria found so offensive, their scant mumbled greetings, their boisterous ways, their door slamming. Which ones would she be calling someday, asking them to pick up a quart of low-fat milk and a loaf of bread?

No, what was she thinking? When that day came, twenty years from now, if she was lucky, those teenagers would be off on their own. It was their parents she should be considering. They'd be just the right age by then—past full-time parenthood, old enough to have subsided into compassion, yet still competent. Maybe she should start cultivating them now. Who else would there be? Jessica would be full of concern, but would she fly in from halfway across the globe to tend to her? Right now she was in Prague. Her husband was in the diplomatic corps; she'd always be far away. When they spoke once a week, the old closeness returned—a sheltering warmth of knowing and being known, a loosening of every taut cell—but when Amanda put the phone down, the warmth dissipated as if she'd shed a fur coat.

As for Ben, most likely any helping would be the other way around. That was the price for having a lover at her age: eventually the woman had to manage the decline. She'd thought of it when they first met two years ago and fell immediately into bed. Did she really want to risk going through all that again? Yes. So far she didn't regret her decision, even though bed was not quite what it had been at the start. A man a decade younger rather than older would be preferable, but that opportunity came up very rarely.

The shop was bustling that day. There was a convention of psychotherapists in a nearby hotel and the women came in groups, chattering, going through the racks and taking turns in the dressing rooms. Her two assistants were overwhelmed and Amanda had to help at the register. The neighborhood was buzzing with the rumor that the landlord was planning to raise the rent: it was only a matter of time before the independent shops would be forced out. This Amanda refused to think about. She telephoned Maria the first chance she got. No change. The pains were still terrible.

"You must call the doctor immediately."

"All right. If I can find the number."

As soon as Amanda got home, the phone rang. Maria must have watched from the peephole or listened for her key in the door.

"The doctor said I have to call an ambulance and go to the hospital as soon as I can."

"So? It's nearly eight o'clock. What are you waiting for?"

"I have to have my dinner first."

"Dinner? With all that pain?"

"I can't go on an empty stomach."

"I'm coming over in half an hour to call the ambulance. Be ready."

Several of the teenagers were standing outside the building as she saw Maria into the ambulance. They nodded and looked appropriately sober; one boy offered to help Amanda with Maria's overnight bag, which was hardly necessary. They probably thought she and Maria were of the same generation—to teenagers everyone over forty looks alike.

Maria had emergency surgery to remove her appendix. Amanda veered between sympathy and rage. If the appendix had burst and been fatal, she would have been the one to find the body when she went in to check. A vague guilt, barely averted this time, hovered nearby.

She visited the hospital every few days on the way home from work, summoning the required good cheer. It was like putting on an old dress she'd never much liked, but was just right for certain occasions—a funeral dress, a job interview dress. Hospital visits to Jack had been easier after he lost consciousness—at least she didn't have to pretend optimism. Maria's progress was slow, the nurses said, not because of the operation, which was successful, but because she wouldn't eat. She sat in a wheelchair and whined about the poor food. She was down to eighty-five pounds, she told Amanda with a perverse pride.

Fortunately there was a social worker in charge now. This was Amanda's busiest time. Christmas wasn't far off: the gift items had to be displayed, and meanwhile she had to go around looking at the designers' spring fashions. She needed to do some shopping for herself as well. It wouldn't do to appear shabby—not that she ever approached shabbiness, but her standards were high.

Nevertheless, when Maria told the social worker that the one thing she enjoyed eating was soup, Amanda made a vegetable soup to welcome her home. The next day Maria reported the soup was "too much," so she'd put it in the freezer. Amanda seethed. What did too much mean, anyway? Quantity? She needn't eat it all at once. Too thick?

Add water. She was sorry now that she hadn't kept any for herself.

Fine, she thought, once you finish starving yourself to death I'll defrost it and have a memorial meal.

December was unusually dark and bleak. The first ring of the phone didn't quite wake her but transformed into a dream: Jack was calling from the hospital, his voice surprisingly strong and deep, as it was when they first met. He asked her to bring him a book about World War II that he'd been reading before his heart attack and wanted to finish before he died. She tried to remember where in the apartment she'd last seen the book: in the freezer, it seemed, but that didn't make any sense. The phone kept ringing, the dream slid away, and Amanda leaped up, thinking how odd that anyone, especially Jack, should want to die with war on his mind. Her hand on the receiver was shaking—she half-expected to hear his voice when she picked up. Instead it was the familiar plaintive whisper.

"I'm sorry to call so early but could you come over right away?"

"Maria? What's wrong? Are you sick?"

"No. I can't tell you over the phone. Could you just come over?"

Her whisper was like the rustle of a mouse. Amanda had to strain to hear. "Do you realize what time it is?" She glanced at the clock. "Five fifty-four. Isn't the aide with you?" Since the surgery, there were aides around the clock.

"She's sleeping. If you could just please come over? And close your door very quietly."

Amanda put on a robe, drank a glass of water, and smoothed down her hair, glancing in the mirror as if something might have changed while she slept. But there was that face again, the face she couldn't believe was her own: tense and ashy without makeup, ringed by hair that was lusterless and awry, a face that warned of things to come. She grabbed her keys and, like a helpless child seeking small ways to show power, didn't close the door quietly as instructed.

Maria's door opened a crack and she motioned Amanda to sidle around the edge. The dim hall smelled like old cooking—dark root vegetables, eggplants, turnips, squash. In the wan light, Maria's bony face was gray-green, the hollows in her cheeks tinged beige. Besides the kerchief tied under her chin, she wore a short filmy white garment that reminded Amanda of Indian holy men with their begging bowls. She had on the black Oxford shoes and white stockings, dotted with holes, that went from her ankles to her knees like dancers' leg warmers; between the stockings and the nightgown was a bare strip of desiccated bluish thigh. Her legs were so narrow that Amanda could have ringed them with her hands. She tried not to stare.

The aides couldn't be trusted, Maria whispered. Things were missing.

"What things?"

"Things. I want you to take something for safekeeping. Come." She shuffled into a small room crammed with ancient furniture and pointed to a two-foot-long metal box on the floor, labeled with her name. "This is my good silver and some other things. I want you to hold it for me."

"Oh, come on. No one's going to make off with that. It must be heavy." She lifted it; it was very heavy. At this hour, for this absurd caprice, patience deserted her. "I was sleeping. Did you really have to wake me for this?" The call from the hospital when Jack died had come at four-seventeen—she remembered the green numbers on the clock. That was in June, the sky already lightening, and she wasn't sleeping well anyway.

"I'm sorry," said Maria. "Don't talk so loud. Will you take it, please?"

"Maria." Ridiculous, this whispering in the dark like conspirators. "You know I'd help you with anything reasonable, but this—this is—"

"Will you take it?" she pleaded.

"All right. But if you keep thinking this way, next thing you'll be accusing me of stealing it. Have you been eating?"

"I'm okay," Maria murmured. "Just a little weak."

"From now on, don't call at this hour unless it's an emergency."

Amanda lugged the box across the hall and stowed it under the bed in Jessica's old room. She didn't want it in sight, reminding her of that cringing imperiousness, those dreadful stockings, the Tinker Toy legs, the whinging voice.

This must not continue, she thought as she climbed back into bed, her insides trembling. Later she'd call the social worker and tell her about the growing paranoia.

But she never did manage to call. The day turned out hectic. An order of cashmere scarves was delayed, one of the assistants was out sick, and a long-time customer made a fuss about returning a suede coat that had obviously been worn. The rumors about the landlord continued, becoming more credible. Just when Amanda thought she might catch her breath, a new customer entered, young, impeccably turned out, flaunting her beauty, and so much like Jessica—the glossy chestnut hair with its nonchalant swing, the broad shoulders and narrow hips and small breasts—that for a mad instant Amanda thought she'd come on a surprise visit and almost dashed over to embrace her. Luckily she caught herself in time. The young woman's fingers flicked swiftly through the clothes on the rack as she frowned in concentration. Clarissa, one of the assistants, greeted her and began the usual routine. Instead of working at her desk in back as usual, Amanda lingered nearby until the woman went into the dressing room with three suits. Later she asked Clarissa if she'd bought anything. No. "I don't think she was really serious. Probably just passing the time before a lunch date." Amanda was so rattled that she had to do the accounts over again; she'd forgotten to save her work on the computer.

She didn't get home till almost nine. The janitor was polishing the brass in the lobby.

"She's gone, your neighbor," he said in greeting. At her puzzled look, he added, "The skinny lady opposite you? An ambulance came at five. Big scene. That's why I'm so late doing this."

"Gone? You mean back to the hospital?"

"Gone like dead."

Amanda's heart thumped, and then came a small ping of relief: thank goodness she hadn't had to deal with it.

"She looked dead already when they loaded her on. Can't nobody live, that thin. I knew when I saw her after the operation. It was only a matter of time."

Isn't it always? she thought. "She's been here for ages, hasn't she?"

"Fifty years. Longest tenant in the building. The super next door, Freddy? He remembers her husband."

"She had a husband?" This was incredible. What could he have been like? Cringing and fearful like her? Or overbearing, a hawk to her sparrow? Immediately she envisioned sex: not possible. Maria being caressed, penetrated? Maria under a man, or sitting on top, bouncing up and down? The chirping sounds she'd manage to squeeze out? The vision was grotesque.

"Yeah, he died maybe thirty years ago," the janitor said. "In a wheelchair by the end. She must've lost her will after that. You need will to go on in this life."

She preferred the super's bluntness to the professional tones of the nurse who'd called about Jack: "We're terribly sorry to tell you Mr. Green has passed on." She could still hear the creamy voice. Four-seventeen, a promising June day.

No more crack-of-dawn phone calls. Well, she would hardly miss those. In fact she wouldn't miss anything about Maria, not even the chance to exercise her own virtue.

And yet Maria would not be quite gone. There was still the box. Upstairs, Amanda dragged it out from under Jessica's bed. The label was written in a spotty ballpoint pen, a marginal improvement on the number 4 pencils. She had no desire to open it, no curiosity, only distaste. Probably she wasn't supposed to open it. There must be a lawyer involved, maybe a distant heir. There'd been a husband; could there be children, grandchildren? Maria had never mentioned any family and seemed never to have visitors. What was it like to pass through life leaving no one, nothing? Would anyone turn up to arrange a funeral service? Someone from the church, maybe. Maria had managed to get there now and then until her appendicitis.

The box could wait. She shoved it back out of sight, then lay down on Jessica's bed as if she, too, were waiting. Shouldn't she be feeling something? Her own callousness distressed her. She hadn't always been this way. When had she changed? In an effort to induce a respectable response, to pierce the numbness surrounding her like a bubble, she tried to picture Maria's last hours, alone except for the aide she distrusted. Pain, maybe. Fear, certainly. She was sorry Maria had had to endure them. But it was a generic sorrow, what she might feel for any living creature. There was nothing that reached inside the bubble, no grief, no loss. Perhaps Maria had drifted off in her sleep. Or had she reached for the phone to call Amanda? She checked the machine again: no messages.

It was useless trying to conjure emotion out of nothing; she need not add hypocrisy to detachment. She changed into a pair of sweatpants, turned on the TV in the kitchen to catch the news, and got busy making a salad.

Two days later, at the shop, she got a call from a lawyer who informed her that she was the heir to the contents of Maria's apartment.

"No. I mean, there must be some mistake. I'm just a neighbor, I . . ."

"I assure you, you're the designated heir. It's in the will."

"The will? But what am I supposed to do with all that stuff? I mean, I don't know what to say. I had no idea she planned to . . ."

"There are places that deal with unwanted items. Auctions, that sort of thing. I can send you some information when I send a messenger with the keys."

"I have her keys. She gave them to me weeks ago."

"I still have to give you the set of keys in my possession."

She told the lawyer about the box. "What am I supposed to do with it? Silver, I think she said. There must be someone . . ."

"There's no one else mentioned in the will. I'm afraid everything in her apartment is now yours." He had a rueful, ironic tone that appealed to her. He understood—he must have known Maria. She wondered what he was like, how old he was.

"What about . . . will there be a funeral?" Surely this

could not fall to her too.

He seemed to read her mind. "Yes, not to worry. The church is handling that."

The conversation was over before she could learn anything about him. They arranged for the messenger and he gave her his phone number in case she had any questions.

Now she could repossess her rejected soup. Ben would enjoy it. But at the thought of the soup a wave of nausea skimmed through her. She wouldn't go so far as to think Maria poisoned it—though the notion did flash by—but she imagined the soup might have soured simply by languishing in the freezer of that unwholesome apartment.

The next day she opened the box. She found an excellent set of silver, service for eight, in an austere, old-fashioned pattern; it needed a good scrubbing and a dose of silver polish. Wrapped in a bit of flannel were a strand of pearls, a plain gold bracelet, and two pairs of earrings, small glittering studs. They looked like costume jewelry but she would have them appraised, to be sure. If they turned out to be worth anything, she'd give the money away; she did not wish to profit from her inheritance. She didn't deserve to profit, because there had been no love. Only kindness. No, even less, acquiescence. She rather liked the silver, but would not use it. It felt... tainted. The word that sprang to mind surprised her. Tainted by what? By solitude, by isolation, and those would not wash off.

She delayed entering the apartment for several days, dreading her task. At last, on a Sunday morning, she unlocked the door and turned on every light. She ripped the drapes from the windows and they settled on the floor in a cloud of dust. Daylight came oozing in, strained by the film of dust coating the windows. She was overcome with desolation. Why had all of this been given to her? Possessing it seemed to taint her with dust as well, with a musty odor of loneliness and decline. It was given to her because there was no one else. Because Maria had appreciated her help. Or perhaps the opposite: a slap in the face, paying back the false kindness in kind. Or was there an even more subtle motive for the bequest, an ironic, taunting message: You, too, someday...

Whatever the motive, Amanda resolved to do the minimum—the dead don't need kindness. Any papers that looked important, she'd give to the lawyer. The rest she wouldn't touch, just make a list, then call one of the places he'd suggested and have it carted away. She could pay the janitor to empty the refrigerator. It was the landlord's job to have the place cleaned for the next tenant. Someone else in her position, she knew, might be eager to go through Maria's things, construct a plausible history or unearth surprising adventures, to understand how a person could come to such a solitary end. But she had no curiosity; she had had none before, and death had not altered her indifference. No matter what she might discover of Maria's past, it had evaporated. Now there was only emptiness.

She stood at the window looking out at the park across the street; the bare branches shook in the winter wind. She rubbed at a small area on the pane to see more clearly, but though her fingers got sticky with dust, the view stayed filmy: too much grime on the outside. Her own past—Jack, Jessica as a child, the beauty that had sustained her—felt like something she had once dreamed. She still had the shop—though maybe not for long if the rumors about the landlord were true—and she had Ben, yet they felt meager compared to what was gone. Insubstantial somehow, like polyester clothes.

One day Jessica would stand gazing out at the same trees, wondering what to do with her mother's possessions. The clothes, the books, the furniture would seem a burden. Though maybe she'd want some of the clothes, all so finely made and carefully chosen. Jessica was more or less the same size, at least when Amanda last saw her. She might have gained weight with the second baby. Later she would phone Jessica. Maria's apartment was chilly; she needed to feel warmth. Love. Not so much Jessica's love—that was dependable, if distant—but her own. Love of the world. She needed her daughter's voice to rouse her into feeling.

Pickup

I was standing in front of my hotel smoking a cigarette because of course no smoking was allowed anywhere in the
building. And in the hospital where my father lay recovering—I hoped—from surgery, forget it. A shiny black car
pulled up and parked right in front of me. It was probably
coming to pick up someone in the hotel. No one came out,
though, and the car stayed parked for several minutes. The
driver seemed to be staring at me, as if wondering whether
I was his passenger.

Or could he possibly think I was hanging out in front
of the hotel looking for a pickup—the other kind of pickup? I certainly was not dressed to entice customers; I was
wearing jeans and sneakers and an old down jacket. They
were good enough for visiting my father in the hospital,
which was why I was at this hotel in this strange city. Had I
been a call girl I would have been dressed quite differently.
Still, he waited.

Suddenly I felt an urge for adventure, for the unfore-
seen. The time spent with my mother and sister, sitting in
the hospital waiting room, managed to be both tense and
monotonous. I meandered over to the car, opened the front
door, and looked at the driver questioningly. He waved me
in. I couldn't help recalling the many times my parents had
warned me not to get into cars with strange men, but I was

an adult now. Being around sickness and death puts one in a devil-may-care mood. I stubbed out the cigarette on the curb, then hesitated, not sure whether to sit in the front or back seat. If he were merely a chauffeur, waiting to deliver me to some exciting encounter, then the back. On the other hand, why not be friendly, just in case? I got into the front seat and he started the engine.

"You're almost too late," he said.

"Hold on! You're not from the hospital, are you? Did something happen?"

"Hospital? I don't know what you're talking about."

"Never mind," I said. "I'm sorry, I was delayed."

"They've had everything all ready for a half hour. They can't start without you."

"They'll just have to wait, then, won't they?" Naturally I wondered who and what he was referring to. He wasn't looking for a pickup, obviously—an available woman, I mean, which I had almost hoped might be the case. But studying him more closely I was glad—he was not the least bit attractive with his shiny balding head and tiny hairs sprouting from his ears, and his stubby fingers on the steering wheel. Maybe I had agreed to a quick gig and forgotten about it in the flurry over my father's surgery, but the TV commercials I appear in—laundry soap, cars, cat food—are almost always shot in New York or Los Angeles. The downtown streets we were passing through were totally unfamiliar. Anyway, I always get a text from my agent a couple of hours ahead as a reminder.

"It's not just the orchestra. The audience is pretty restless."

There was never an audience for a commercial shoot, and the music was prerecorded. "But you just got here yourself."

"You were supposed to take a taxi. When you didn't answer your phone they sent me out."

I took out my phone and saw that I had forgotten to turn the ringer back on after I went to a movie last night. Dinner with the family in an awful Italian restaurant had been trying and I'd needed distraction. I couldn't even remember what I had seen. It might have involved a kidnapping.

"Look," I said finally, "I'm totally confused. Maybe you can explain what this is all about, where we're headed."

He handed me a printed program for a concert taking place that night at the Town Hall, featuring a pianist playing one of the Rachmaninoff concertos with the local orchestra. My name was on it. Also there was a photo that looked a good deal like me but wasn't me. Something about the lips and chin was not quite right. Not to mention that this woman looked older than I thought I looked.

"There's been some mistake. That's not me. I'm not a pianist." True, I had taken piano lessons as a young girl and in fact was quite good, so good that my high-school teachers urged me to continue and apply to one of the well-known music conservatories. But I didn't want to. My dream was to study acting, which I did, not that it has gotten me anywhere past laundry soap thus far. Often those commercials lead to real acting work but in my case that hasn't happened yet. Maybe I should have stuck to the piano.

At a red light he snatched the program back. "Are you..." And he read the name on the program, which was my name. At least it had been my name for as long as I could remember. I was getting so flustered I could barely remember who I was. This can occur, for instance, after my portrayal of a housewife thrilled with her new laundry soap is so convincing that I convince myself, and for a short while after, I feel I'm that nonexistent woman.

"Yes, I am, but I'm not a pianist, I told you. I'm an actor.

This photo looks a lot like me but it isn't quite me. I should know, shouldn't I? Someone got the names mixed up. Maybe she's staying at the same hotel."

"Well, it's too late to go back for her now. They're expecting us. You'll just have to go through with it." He slowed down and turned off the wide avenue we were traversing into a side street.

"But . . . but . . . I'm not dressed for it. Look at me."

He looked down at my jeans and sneakers disdainfully. "They'll give you something to wear. Sometimes performers leave their gowns in the dressing room. Or you can get a dress from one of the violinists—there are so many, one less won't make any difference."

"But the shoes . . ." I murmured.

He didn't answer. We were approaching a large white classical building; people milled around outside. The driver pulled into the parking lot behind it.

"Get a move on. Any longer and they might have to cancel."

Cancel! That could be my way out. But he opened my door, grabbed me by the arm and dragged me in through the back entrance, where several men in formal wear took me in hand and talked all at once so I couldn't get a word in. A woman appeared, holding a blue gown over her arm, and hustled me into a dressing room, where she practically tore off my clothes and left them in a heap on the floor. Before I knew it, I was in the dress, which fit perfectly—I could see in the mirror. She even had a pair of black pumps, low-heeled so I wouldn't trip getting on and offstage. She hastily dabbed some makeup on my face and smoothed down my hair—all this took only about three minutes—then handed me back to the waiting men.

"Wonderful to have you with us at last," one said, patting me lightly on the shoulder. "Break a leg."

I was practically pushed onstage, blinking in the bright lights, where I moved toward the piano and bowed, as I had seen performers do. The conductor approached to shake my hand. There were sheets of music on the piano—they would certainly help; I'd always been a good sight-reader—and a page turner, a young woman in black who smiled encouragingly at me. While the audience applauded my entrance, I tried to get my head together. My father, who lay recovering from his surgery, as I kept hoping, had told me when I was a child, Whatever life calls upon you to do, concentrate and do it the best you can. That's all anyone can expect of you.

I had heard the concerto a few times and knew when the piano came in. I found the place on the page in front of me. I lowered my hands to the keys and waited. Then it was time for my opening notes. I hesitated a split second, and began. Soon the orchestra joined me, and together we performed the music. I did the best I could, and apparently it was good enough, or even better than that, because at the end the audience rose to their feet and clapped. Fortunately that was the only piece I was expected to play; the rest was a suite of Hungarian folk dances and, finally, a Brahms symphony.

Back in the dressing room I hastily called the hospital to check on my father. I had planned to go there after I smoked my cigarette in front of the hotel, but now it was too late. Visiting hours were almost over. When she heard it was me, the head nurse on his floor said, "Where have you been? Your family is worried about you."

"I'm fine. Something came up. But how is he?" I asked impatiently.

"Oh, everything went well. He's awake and responding. Tomorrow we might even get him up on his feet."

I burst into tears of relief.

"Take it easy," she said. "Come tomorrow and see for yourself. 'Bye now."

I hastily composed myself because three of the men in formal dress entered to congratulate me and lead me on-stage for a curtain call. I was given lavish bouquets of flowers. Tomorrow I would take them to the hospital.

Return of the Frenchman

I was wandering through the vast reaches and crannies of the enormous supermarket, which was reorganized every week so that it was hard to find even the most ordinary items, such as romaine lettuce, for which I searched to no avail. I gave up and decided to buy a loaf of bread, since I was standing right near the bread counter and the baker was smiling invitingly. I asked for a baguette and he said he'd have to go in the back and get it, they were just coming out of the oven. A man appeared beside me, very smartly dressed in summer whites, a straw hat with a black band on his head. I'll take one too, he said. The baker nodded and disappeared into the back.

The man turned to face me and smiled. "Will you come away with me now?" he asked.

I was so startled I almost fell over. What could one possibly say to such a proposal from a stranger in the supermarket? He must have seen the shock on my face for he added, "Why not? My car is just around the corner. We can stop off for your passport."

Of course, I couldn't consider doing such a preposterous thing, but a change did come over me at his peculiar logic. Why not indeed? With his hat and white clothes he was quite dashing. Why all the formalities and complexities attendant upon two people getting together?

At that moment the baker appeared with our baguettes and placed them in long bags. We each took a bag and I turned to go. The man said, "A missed opportunity, yet again," and then he touched his hat and walked away towards the cleaning supplies.

"Wait," I called after him. "What do you mean, again?"

"Don't you remember that dinner party some years ago?"

That was when I realized it was the Frenchman, come back. In fact he had spoken with a very faint accent, which I hadn't noticed because of my shock. Also, he had said very few words.

The dinner party he alluded to took place a few years ago when I was in my early thirties and happily, if sometimes agitatedly, married. Along with my husband and me were several other guests, including a French banker. He seemed a few years older than I and was probably with a wife or companion, whom I've totally forgotten. He was fairly tall, very trim and well built, and he wore a white dress shirt open at the collar, no tie; the white of his shirt was gleaming, whiter than white. It contrasted with his olive skin and his very black straight hair, almost like Indian hair. He spoke excellent English, only a very slight accent.

My feelings were unsettling: I was so drawn to this man that if he had taken me aside and asked me to run away with him that very night, I would have done so without hesitating. As we had drinks before dinner I imagined him finding an excuse to whisper to me privately in the hall, suggesting a time and place for our elopement. We could arrange to leave the party together and grab a taxi to the airport. (Though I would have to go home for my passport, and so, most likely, would he. So an arrangement for tomorrow might be better.) The presence of my husband did not deter me from my fantasies, although I loved him. The intensity of my feelings for this unknown Frenchman erased all other connections.

He participated in the dinner-table conversation graciously and intelligently. I wondered if he was having the same feelings for me as I was for him. After dinner, as we all sat around in the living room drinking coffee, I imagined he was addressing his remarks to me in particular, but I couldn't be sure. It would have suited my fantasies better had he spoken with a stronger French accent.

The only drawback to our future life together was that he was a banker. I had negative attitudes about bankers for all the usual reasons. I wouldn't want to be closely associated with one, just as I wouldn't wish to be closely allied with a petty criminal or a con man. But the magnetic pull I felt towards him overcame any reservations. It didn't matter what he was or did. Maybe he was a good banker, the kind that gave loans to poor homeowners, or helped fund small third-world businesses.

The evening was pleasant enough, as such evenings go—the food was good, the conversation lively, the hosts gracious. We all said good night; probably I shook hands with the banker and even the woman he was with. It didn't occur to me to catch him in a corner and suggest we meet somewhere for coffee in the next few days, maybe invent some reason we should meet again, advice about investments, say. I didn't know then how such things were managed. Even *if* they were managed. I accepted that I would never see him again. Really, I'd known all evening that my fantasies would remain fantasies. I was even hoping that by the end of the dinner party he would have said or done something unforgivable that would destroy the magnetism that yanked me towards him and that I resisted by an effort of will. But he didn't. He remained perfect.

Had I been someone else, or had I been able to pretend I was someone else, I could have managed future meetings. But I wasn't someone else. I had set into who I was, like a cake batter poured into a mold. I'd never developed the imagination for such adventures. Since then I've learned that many things I used to think were impossible are quite possible.

And now the banker had reappeared. Obviously his notion of the possible was considerably broader than mine. Once again I'd let the opportunity slip away. If I had recognized him right away, would I have responded differently? Now he was lost in the cleaning supplies section, and though I pushed my cart swiftly through those aisles, I couldn't find him.

I consoled myself by thinking maybe he wasn't even the same man. Just an impudent stranger.

The Strong One

The red light on the phone machine was blinking when she came in from work. Seductive, and like all things seductive, it brought mixed feelings. She'd been vaguely hoping, lately, for an event, something to enliven her. Or something to look forward to. Although the peace of nothing happening did have its appeal. Her older daughter, Isabel, once told her that her Hello sounded like What now?

It was a message from Isabel: Call back when you have a chance. Very casual. Still, Caroline thought she detected a slight edge to the voice. Maybe one of the kids was sick again, or her husband's back was acting up. She might even have called to check on her parents. In the last year or so Isabel had shown a solicitude Caroline found premature, yet she didn't discourage it. There might come a time when they'd need it.

She put down her briefcase, kicked off her shoes—the sensible shoes she hated; she couldn't walk in high heels anymore—and lay down on the couch. She'd call back soon. Tiredness plagued her these days. More tedium than tiredness.

Events, welcome and unwelcome, used to roll out like an endless rug under her feet, till she would long for a bit of stillness. Now that she had her stillness, it left her restless, expectant. She wasn't officially retired; she taught one or two advanced math courses but was relieved of the departmental chores. She might come across the occasional promising doctoral candidate, or a knotty problem that absorbed her. Recently one of her articles had been selected for a prestigious anthology—that was an event of sorts. But she no longer anticipated elation from her work. Mathematicians peak early; her time was past. In a few years the administration might begin offering her tempting retirement packages. That would feel humiliating but she was prepared to accept it. The humiliations that had settled on her face and body were harder to accept.

For she was old; there was no way she could consider herself middle-aged anymore. Older than people thought—her colleagues, her neighbors, her friends. Or so she hoped. She took excellent care of herself, of every part she had the slightest control over. She was careful about her clothes, her posture—that forward tilt older people developed was a dead giveaway. It was only the shoes that betrayed her. But she knew how old she was. Very soon people might start saying, or thinking, She looks very good for her age: the ultimate insult. When Ivan was in the hospital for his heart operation four years ago, the surgeon had referred to the operation as an insult. "It's the second insult," he said. "What was the first?" Caroline asked. "The first insult," the surgeon said, "is birth." She had not had any major surgery. Her second insult was age.

She didn't even care about sex anymore. Well, no, that was not quite accurate. She liked it all right. It had always gone well with her and Ivan, was probably what had kept them together for so long, through years of turbulence. But now she could take it or leave it, and rarely thought about it except when it was happening. Sometimes it felt like one more domestic chore to get done before falling off to sleep.

As with cooking, there was a payoff in the end, but it lasted so short a time, and when it was over, that was that. The warm physical hum she used to feel for hours afterward had deserted her.

The children were embarked on their adult lives; she and Ivan no longer lay awake fretting over Isabel and Greta—their choices and habits, their periodic crises and commotions, the latter more Greta's than Isabel's. Isabel, who had been an easy child, was an architect and so was her husband, Neil; between them they ran a thriving practice in Brooklyn, the new Mecca. Isabel's children, the doted-on grandchildren, would move from stage to stage, providing keen pricks of delight, like the five-year-old's birthday party with the magician and face painter. But those delights did not spear Caroline through and through. They were replays of things that had happened before: first mouthful of cereal, first word, first step, first day of school . . .

Greta, always the more volatile daughter, remained erratic, but her unpredictability had grown so predictable that it was no longer alarming. Greta had moved on from a childhood of playing with matches and jumping into deep water to an adolescence hectic with drugs and sex, but miraculously nothing too terrible had come of this. When some years ago Caroline and Ivan sat on the sunny green lawn at her college graduation—delayed a year while Greta backpacked in Europe—Caroline thought with relief that they had gotten her through.

At last she got up and phoned Isabel.

"Everything's fine," Isabel said. "I just thought I should tell you—well, the doctor found a lump in my breast. She says it may be nothing serious, but I have to go for a mammogram and maybe a biopsy. Usually they don't do that till you're forty but—do you think you could pick up the kids at school tomorrow? I hate to ask, but—"

"Wait a minute. What did she say exactly?" Her heart was pounding.

"Only what I said. She felt something. I can barely feel it myself. It's probably nothing. Even with a mammogram—there are so many false positives. That's the trouble with these—"

"But did she sound alarmed?"

"I told you, Mom," Isabel said patiently. "She just said I needed the tests. So about tomorrow . . . It's not one of your teaching days, is it? I'd have Mark do it but he has basketball practice and I'd hate for him to miss it."

Of course she would pick up the children. Mark, who was twelve, could come home himself later. The girls were seven and five.

"Unless you want to get a sitter and I could go to the doctor with you . . . ?" Caroline suggested.

"Thanks, but Neil is coming with me."

It must be serious if Neil was giving up an afternoon of work. Isabel must be more frightened than she let on. Of course she was frightened. Terrified. Who wouldn't be? Caroline hung up but was too jittery to lie down again. She went into her study and tried correcting exam papers, but it was no use.

Why couldn't it have been her? She'd willingly substitute. Last year they attended the funeral of a neighbor's seven-year-old who'd been hit by a car. His grandmother wept and moaned, "Why couldn't it have been me? I'm old enough." "Because you don't ride a bike," someone had murmured.

Caroline's mind was whirring from terror. She had always been prone to fantasy, unraveling possibilities the way she unraveled math riddles. Already she was picturing the worst. The ghastly treatments, the slow fading... No, Isabel couldn't die, she shouted silently. It simply couldn't happen; it would be too cruel.

She must stop this, the fantasies, the anticipation. Nothing had happened yet. She'd always been fiercely protective of her children—too much so, Ivan thought. Maybe it was because she had imagined she'd never have any. It had taken a long time to conceive Isabel. They had thought it would never happen, and then it did. Greta came much more easily, unplanned, accidental.

This was no time to give in to weakness. She had to be strong when she told Ivan. In the morning he'd mentioned what time he'd be home. He had an appointment about his new project of bringing art exhibits to depressed neighborhoods in special vans. He was wrapped in a towel after his shower, and as usual she had taken pleasure in his leanness, the body she'd loved for so long and that didn't show its years nearly as much as her own. She remembered exactly how he looked, but forgot what time he said.

She'd better call Greta too. The girls were close; maybe she already knew. Where was Greta today, anyway, with her crazy schedule? Greta bounced from one enthusiasm to another—for a while she'd performed with a modern dance troupe, then worked at a shelter for abused women; she had dipped into Buddhism but couldn't sit still to meditate, and then anarchism, attending rallies and passing out leaflets. Now she taught English as a second language and, she recently told her parents, was preparing to become a personal trainer. There had been men on and off, break-ups and the attendant sagas. Caroline and Ivan learned not to become too attached to these men, as they might not last long. The current man was Seth, a money manager at a small corporation, whom in her anarchist period Greta would have scorned. But they seemed to get along well. It was a year and a half since she had moved into his large apartment, and from what Caroline could observe, Greta appreciated the change after her rickety, overpriced studio in the East Village. Maybe she would stay with him simply for the ease of it.

She was not strong when Ivan came home. She collapsed in tears and he had to be the strong one, holding her, reassuring her.

"We don't even know what it is yet. It's too soon to get frantic. Let's wait and see what the tests show."

"I'm sorry. I didn't mean to tell you like this."

"Don't apologize. We'll get through it. She will. Remember all the things we've managed to get through?"

"But not breast cancer."

"Don't suffer in advance, sweetheart. Try to keep yourself together."

"Okay, I'll try."

The next few weeks did not lack for events. There were the doctors' appointments and tests, the children to be seen to. Isabel allowed Caroline to accompany her to get the results of the biopsy. Neil came too. Caroline sat with him in the waiting room leafing through a copy of *Vogue* while he did a crossword puzzle. After a short time the doctor waved Neil into the office, but not Caroline.

When he came out alone a few minutes later, his normally ruddy face was greenish. He was a tall, hefty man of forty-one, but he seemed to have shrunk a few inches and aged a few years. A clump of his shirt was hanging over his belt.

"It's bad, isn't it?" she said. She remembered Ivan's words. She had to be strong. Neil was suffering—she must be calm for his sake.

He nodded. Caroline had known from the very first. Maybe even when she heard Isabel's edgy voice on the answering machine. Was that possible?

"Sit," she told him. "You look like you're going to fall down. I'll get you some water? So are they going to remove the breast?"

He shook his head. "The doctor isn't sure yet. She'll study the tests and consult with someone else. Maybe they can do a lumpectomy."

She got him a cup of water from the machine across the room. "Which breast is it, anyway?" she asked. How odd that she should be talking about Isabel's breasts with her son-in-law. Isabel's body was no longer in her care, as in the early years when Caroline felt she had to guard it— flesh of her flesh. Now the breasts were part of her intimate life with Neil. She'd been surprised when Isabel first introduced him, Isabel who was quietly able and understated. Neil's intensity and self-assurance had been off-putting, but Caroline had grown to love him. If his life were in danger she would grieve, surely, but not with this cold shuddering in her blood. She wrapped her sweater around herself to make it stop.

"The right," he said, looking surprised. "Why?"

"I don't know. It just occurred to me."

She thought Isabel might stumble out of the doctor's office and fall into her arms. She was ready. But Isabel's step was firm, and instead she grasped Neil's arm. "Let's go home." Then, with barely a glance at Caroline, "He told you?"

"Yes. You'll be all right, I know. We'll all take care of you. Go on, I'll get a cab home." She wanted to cradle Isabel in her arms, but she could tell they wanted to be alone.

That night she told Ivan the news. She hadn't seen him weep since his mother died six years ago. There had been tears at a couple of awful moments in their long marriage. And right after Isabel was born, he sat at the edge of her hospital bed stroking her hair, smiling broadly and wiping a few tears from his eyes. Now he sat bent over at the kitchen table with his head in his hands.

Caroline tried to soothe him. "She'll be all right. I know she will."

"How do you know?" he said almost angrily. "They say there's a five-year life expectancy after breast cancer."

"They do?"

"Yes."

"That must be an old statistic. They do these things better now." She stroked his shoulder. "Look, let's order a pizza."

"Aren't you frightened?" he asked. "A few days ago you were falling apart."

"I'm still scared. But I don't want to let it get the better of me. Then I'll be useless. You said to be strong. Now you be strong."

"Oh, don't put on your competent act," he muttered.

It's not an act, she thought.

"I'm sorry," he said. "Remember when she was born? They were afraid the cord might be wrapped around her neck? After all our waiting."

This was too much. She got up and sat on his lap, stroked his hair as if he were a child.

While they sat in the kitchen they heard the doorbell and then Greta entered with her key. "It's just me," she called. "Oh, I was afraid I'd find you like this," she said, tossing her coat on a kitchen chair. She put her arms around them. "She'll be fine. She's young and strong and the doctors have so much experience with these surgeries. And they have some new medication now that prevents a recurrence."

"Hi, sweetheart," Caroline said, getting up off Ivan's lap, mildly embarrassed to be found there, but Greta didn't seem to notice. She must have come straight from a dance class, or maybe it was yoga. She was wearing blue tights and a black leotard, with some sort of Mexican-looking tunic over them. There was something different since they had seen her last, about two weeks ago. Yes, it was the new blonde streaks in her hair. And could that be a tinge of blue mixed in?

"I'm glad you came. Sit down and tell us what you've been up to. It'll be a change."

"First I want to order a pizza. I'm starved after class and it's past nine. I bet you two haven't eaten." She wiped Ivan's wet face with the bottom of her tunic.

"That's just what we were thinking of," Caroline said.

"Dad, she'll be all right. Really. We'll all get her through."

He didn't answer, but put an arm around her waist.

Greta was taking care of her Aged Ps, Caroline thought. It was an old joke the girls had taken from *Great Expectations* when they read it in high school. The Aged P was a half-demented, deaf old father whose devoted son took good care of him.

Reading her mind, Greta said, "Okay, Aged Ps. Mushrooms, anchovies, what?"

The date of the surgery was set. As with Ivan's heart surgery, the waiting was excruciating. Back then, Caroline was impatient to have it over with, to have Ivan fixed and home. She had been the strong one and he had been terrified. Two nurses practically had to drag him from the waiting area. Now, however awful the wait, she wished the day would never come. For the time being Isabel was intact. Caroline was curious to feel the lump. Doctors can make mistakes; maybe it was nothing, a fatty deposit. But with Isabel so silent and pale, she didn't dare ask. She postponed classes to pick up the children while Isabel continued to go to work. Greta sat on the floor with her nieces and cut out paper flowers for a school project.

Caroline and Ivan made love with an urgency they hadn't felt in a long time. Every night he would grasp her hungrily as if they were new lovers who couldn't get enough of each other's flesh or get it fast enough. It was rage at life driving him, or desperation, she thought. She felt rage too, that this should happen. She wanted to keep him inside her as long as she could; when he slipped out she felt abandoned, incomplete. Afterwards he would run his hands over her body inquisitively, the way he had when they first met, as if he were discovering her all over again. She was aroused and they made love again, wearily. Sometimes Ivan would cry, and she held him.

"She's not dead," Caroline said. "You're acting as if she's already dead. It's surgery. They'll fix her."

"I know. I don't know what's come over me. I'm scared." Never in all their years together had he admitted to being frightened, not when Greta had a concussion from a window frame falling on her head, and not when she was fourteen and didn't come home from a friend's party until five in the morning. At the sound of her key in the door Caroline wanted to smack her, but restrained herself. People didn't do that anymore. She could be arrested for child abuse. Although she felt like the one abused.

She thought constantly of death. Two professors at the university had died of breast cancer, but they were almost twice Isabel's age. Still . . . She wondered if Isabel was thinking of death. She must be, even if it didn't show. Isabel was pretending to be strong, but Caroline knew her too well to trust the performance.

She tried to recall how Isabel had first learned about death. How did most children learn? Some lost a pet; a few even lost parents. Movies and television programs showed ample scenes of death; without death there could be no great movies. Did she ever talk to her about mortality the way she remembered talking about sex? She had begun with animals, then worked her way to human bodies. Isabel accepted the information in her calm way, though she did seem a trifle surprised. But death? When had she realized her own life would have an end? Did it frighten her? When Isabel was about nine she and Caroline had passed a homeless man lying wrapped in a blanket on a street corner. Was he dead? she asked. So she knew even then. No, said Caroline, he's just sleeping. She felt ashamed, in her daughter's presence, that she didn't do anything to help. But what could she do?

Caroline's malaise was forgotten. There was too much to think about. She was concerned about Ivan, who wasn't sleeping much. She'd seen a film about a man who lost his job and was so afraid to tell his family that he got suited up every morning and went out, briefcase in hand, to walk the streets or sit in the park. Caroline called Ivan's office at the museum every day on some trivial pretext and was relieved to hear him answer the phone.

Museums were an ideal place to wander for hours. Maybe that was what he did. They were also an ideal place to meet attractive art lovers. Well, if he needed something like that to get him through these weeks, all right, she could live with it. Just now it seemed unimportant. It had happened before, to both of them, when it was important, though she rarely thought about those times now. Greta, an art lover like her father, had met Seth at a museum. Caroline imagined it was Greta who approached first. Well, what did it matter? Seth was like part of the family; he and Greta took Mark to a basketball game over the weekend, to keep him occupied.

The morning of the surgery Caroline's strength drained from her. "I can't. I just can't go," she said to Ivan. "I'll stay in bed and you can call me."

"Of course you can go." Suddenly he was the strong one. "She'll be fine, just like you keep telling me."

"But they're cutting into her. There'll be blood." She buried her face in the pillow.

"It's to make her better." He pulled the covers off the bed and took hold of her arm. "Come on, up. What is it? Do you feel faint?"

"I don't know."

He was already dressed, in jeans and a gray sweater she had gotten him. She resented how attractive she still found him. She wanted to feel nothing, just sleep and have it all be over when she woke. She didn't fear Isabel would die during the surgery; she feared for later.

"It'll all be done in a few hours. Get up." He tugged at her arm.

"Okay, but if I'm not out of the shower soon, come and look for me."

Outside, he helped her into a cab as if she were the sick one. They sat in the waiting room along with the other tense families. Ivan slumped in his chair. Several people fiddled with their phones. A teenaged girl with African braids was staring at an iPad and another was bent over a coloring book. There was a young bearded man Caroline thought she had had in a lecture course a while ago; she hoped he wouldn't notice her. Sunlight streamed in through the windows and the river flowed restlessly outside. Only Neil kept going in and out, for coffee, for a walk, to make a phone call.

The doctor came out smiling. The news was good. They hadn't had to remove the breast, he said, only take out the lump. The prognosis seemed good too. They had to wait for results, but it looked like it hadn't spread. Still, they'd need to keep a close watch. There might be radiation treatments or chemotherapy down the road. Down the road? Caroline winced. What fucking road? The road of life? They could see Isabel in an hour or so but shouldn't be surprised if she was groggy.

"Now we can all go out for lunch," said Seth.

"Are you kidding?" said Caroline. "Could you really eat?"

"I could. I'm starving," said Ivan, beaming as if he were the proud father of a newborn. He was no longer slumped over, and looked as if he had grown a few inches.

Caroline was slightly dizzy but didn't want to say so. Greta noticed, took her arm and propelled her forward. "Just a little while longer, Mom. Here, have a drink." She was never without a bottle of water. "Soon you can see her. It's all over. It's good. And Seth and I have something to tell you. Nice news."

They're getting married, she guessed. She almost said it aloud, but thought better of it.

"What news?" Ivan said.

Greta grinned mischievously. "We'll tell you once we sit down."

"Where's Neil?" Caroline asked at the elevator.

He had disappeared. Ivan went to look and brought

him back from the men's room, where he had evidently gone to weep. He was usually so full of talk, but he didn't say a word, just blinked his bleary eyes.

Greta was pregnant. She announced it shyly, while she and Seth clasped hands on top of the plastic menus. Their faces glowed.

Ivan was delighted and raised his beer in a toast. Neil smiled wanly. Caroline gulped her black coffee and did her best to look pleased—she *was* pleased. She was. It would be wonderful when it happened. But the images of slender Greta with a big belly, Greta cradling an infant, blurred like a vanishing rainbow, beside the ravages of chemotherapy: Isabel sick, weak, losing her splendid dark hair . . .

After a pause she said, "I thought you were going to say you were getting married."

"Well, that might happen someday," Greta said blithely. "One thing at a time."

Isabel looked ashen and limp, the way people look after being heavily drugged and sliced into. Caroline pictured the knife making its first cut, and clutched her own chest. Isabel recognized them and smiled. They stood back so Neil could be close to her.

"She's still so beautiful," Ivan murmured to Caroline and put his arm around her.

"Am I?" Isabel said. "I'm alive, anyway."

On the way home Ivan was giddy with relief while Caroline moved in a haze of apprehension. The dulled feeling was gone for good. Something had finally happened.

Once inside, Ivan put his arms around her and said, "Let's go lie down."

"Yes. But only to rest. I'm not up for anything strenuous."

He gave a faint smile. "No, that's what I meant too."

She lay there wishing she could believe in some far-fetched religion, could prepare magic infusions out of herbs, muttering phrases to the ancestral gods. But there was nothing to do except watch. For the rest of her life she would be watching Isabel, but she must never show it. Unless she herself died before anything bad happened. But though she was old, she was not that old.

They lay side by side, holding hands. Caroline longed to hear reassuring words, but Ivan seemed to have fallen asleep. When she looked more closely, she saw tears seeping from his eyes.

"I thought you were okay. Why suddenly . . . ?"

"I don't know. The whole thing just hit me. That we could lose her."

"No, we can't lose her. I'm so exhausted. Come on, you be the strong one."

"No, you," he said.

The Middle Child

I was starting to recover myself, not quite so heavy of spirit and steeped in gloom, as if occupied by a hostile foreign power. And I noticed this familiar-looking girl hanging around our house, eating with us, playing with our children. I couldn't say how long she'd been there, I just had a vague memory of having seen her before. She appeared about nine or so, and was slightly taller than both of our daughters, who were seven and eleven. She was slender, with long dark wavy hair tied in a scrunchy at the back of her neck. The hair was thick and looked like it could use a combing. She was a quiet child, not sullen, but of a somber disposition. Gloomy, not unlike me.

At first I thought she must be a friend of my older daughter who'd come to visit. Then it struck me that since she was around all the time, slept in the spare bedroom, ate her meals with us, and played with our daughters, she might be part of our family. And yet I didn't remember her. I fed and sheltered her but realized, guiltily, that I never really spoke to her, except to say the most banal things—would you like eggs or cereal for breakfast?—as I would to one of my daughters' friends. As a matter of fact I would have spoken more warmly to one of their friends, tried to draw her out and make her feel at home. With this girl, I never spoke about anything of importance.

I asked my older daughter her name and age—I was embarrassed to ask the girl herself, since clearly I ought to know her—and my daughter said her name was Mary and she was a younger sister, almost nine, which would make her a middle child in our family. Naturally this stunned me. I had no memory of being pregnant in between having our two girls. Was it possible that I'd gone through an entire pregnancy and delivery and not remember it? No, surely my condition hadn't been that bad. Or had it? My daughter, noting my confusion, explained that we had adopted Mary a year ago. This information brought a measure of relief, but even more puzzlement.

I had no memory of the adoption, why or how it had taken place. In bed later that night I asked my husband if this was true, if we had indeed adopted Mary a year ago. He said yes. When I asked how come, he seemed reluctant to give a direct answer. Finally I said, Was it the time when I was so depressed and they wanted to send me to the hospital but I refused?

Well, yes, he said, after a pause.

Did you think another child would cheer me up? I asked with a touch of sarcasm. Or maybe keep me so busy that I wouldn't have time to mope around or lie on the couch with my face to the wall?

Well, sort of, he admitted.

At first I was angry that he had taken such an enormous step, a step that would so alter our lives, without consulting me. But I did consult you, he said. You didn't object. You signed the papers.

I tried to remember how I'd felt during that period, so heavy that I could barely move. I went through the motions of daily life in a fog, always tired, doing what needed to be done, and often barely that. Some of this heaviness was still with me, but a good deal less, as if I had lost pounds of misery.

I fell asleep and dreamed about Mary. In the dream she was smiling and bouncing around like my other children, her sisters. The next morning I woke with a lightness I remembered from years ago, as if sleep had stripped me still further and transported me back to a better time. Every routine that had felt arduous was simple, waking the children for school, preparing breakfast, and so on. Mary was the last to get up, silent and gloomy as usual. Not sullen or hostile, only gloomy.

I took her aside and spoke to her. Mary, I said, let me comb your hair. I took a comb and started going through the tangles while she stood obedient and docile, though it must have hurt. It hadn't been combed out in some time, although it was clean enough. Would you like braids or a ponytail, or should I just leave it loose?

Leave it loose, she said.

It's snowing outside. Do you have a warm winter coat? I asked.

Yes, she said, Dad got it for me, and she pointed to a navy blue down coat hanging on a hook near the door.

When I was done with the hair I said, Mary, my child, can you ever forgive me?

She put her arms around me. I've been waiting for you for so long, she said, and we wept.

Public Transit

My demise started with a little incident on the Broadway bus recently. I was on my way downtown to buy a new bathroom scale, since I suspected that the one I had was no longer accurate. I thought I weighed more than the scale indicated. Sometimes the weight was so low as to be absurd. Though I knew the numbers were wrong, they made me feel I was losing solidity; something was escaping me.

It was early afternoon, a time when the bus is fairly empty, and I was sitting on the window side of the third row of double seats with my backpack on the seat beside me, reading an article about Vietnam veterans, how badly treated they were when they returned, compared to the respect given to veterans of the Iraq war. A middle-aged man got on the bus; he was around forty and carried a shopping bag from a local supermarket. He looked around at the available seats—and there were many—then came straight to the pair of seats I occupied and said, Excuse me, may I sit down? He meant for me to move my backpack.

There are more than a dozen empty seats you could occupy, I said, trying to sound polite though his request was inexplicable. Wouldn't that be easier than having me move my backpack?

But I want to sit in this seat, he said.

I'm sorry, I said, but it seems foolish for me to hold my backpack on my lap when there are so many empty seats.

Foolish or not, this is the seat I want.

Well, I'm not about to give it to you.

This is a public bus and I'm entitled to any empty seat I choose.

Yes, but your request makes no sense. You'd be more comfortable and have more room in the seats in front of me, or in back. Both are empty.

It's none of your business to tell me where I'd be comfortable, he said. His voice was beginning to rise and the few other passengers were staring at us.

All right then, I said, realizing I was dealing with one of the numerous lunatics who ride the buses. The odd thing was that he didn't look like a lunatic. He was well dressed, in a sports jacket and slacks, clean-shaven, and his hair was neatly combed. All right, I repeated, I'll move. If you'll just step aside I'll find another seat.

But he wouldn't move. That's not necessary, he said. I'm not asking you to change your seat. I just want this empty one.

He was blocking my way out of the seat. If you don't move aside, I said, I'll call the driver.

Yes? And tell him what? he said. That you refuse to remove your backpack from the seat so another passenger can sit there?

I'll tell him you're preventing me from changing my seat.

We were both talking quite loudly by now. Some passengers were looking uncomfortable, and it seemed they were beginning to take sides.

Move over, pal, and let the lady get out, one man said from across the aisle.

Oh, hold the goddamn backpack and let him sit down. What's the big deal?

These differing sentiments were expressed in various tones and volumes and accents. People even began to argue among themselves about our situation. The clamor of voices was becoming quite loud.

What's going on back there? the driver called out. Will you all keep quiet so I can concentrate on driving this bus?

There's a guy bothering this lady, called out an older man from the rear.

I beg your pardon, my tormentor said. I'm not bothering her at all. I'm simply asking her to allow me to exercise my rights.

Driver, I said, this man will not allow me to change my seat.

Move over, buddy, and leave the lady alone, said the driver. And please cut out all this commotion.

At this the man moved over with a sweeping, mock-courtly gesture. Go right ahead and change your seat. But if you put your backpack on the seat next to you I'll have to ask if I can sit there.

What's the deal? I said, moving to the empty double row in front of us. Do you have something against backpacks on seats or what? Sure I'd move it if the bus was crowded. But this is crazy, this is a half-empty bus.

Lady, said one exasperated woman right in front of us, will you let it go and let the guy sit where he wants and give us all a break?

I don't see any reason I should do that, I said, and sitting down in the row in front, I placed my backpack on the seat before the man could get to it.

Two teenaged girls were sitting across the aisle and giggling. Which one is crazier? I heard one murmur to the other. And I realized that some of my fellow passengers considered me as nutty as the man who wanted my seat. Maybe I am, I thought. Am I crazy too, or have I just been made crazy by him?

Finally I stood up, took my backpack, and moved towards the rear exit. Here, I said, you can have this seat, or any one you want. I'm going to write to the MTA about this. I got off the bus. It was several stops before mine but I was upset at all the attention. It made me doubt myself. Surely the man was crazy. But had I been too stubborn? Should I have given in right away, as soon as I realized he was not about to yield? I had clung tenaciously to my principles. But clinging to principles may be a kind of madness, in the face of an inexplicable and relentless need.

*   *   *

A few weeks later, another disturbing incident occurred. The young girl sitting in front of me on the bus was disarmingly pretty in a pink-and-gold sort of way. She had glossy honey-colored hair that drifted over the back of her seat, a mere few inches from me. I imagined reaching out and touching it with two fingertips, smelling it. It might have struck the other passengers as odd, had anyone cared, that I'd chosen a seat directly in back of someone, especially someone whose hair intruded on what was technically my space, when the bus was half empty and many more solitary seats were available. People on buses usually sit as far away from one another as they can. They sit close to a stranger only if there are no other options, or they have some ulterior motive. In my case, the choice of seat might have had something to do with the proximity of the hair.

A mid-thirtyish man with a two-day growth of beard and carrying a canvas book bag entered and sat down right beside the girl with the hair. Considering the number of empty seats, this was even odder than my choice. I was immediately suspicious. He began speaking to her in a very low voice; I couldn't make out what he said. She acknowledged him with the smallest possible smile, a mere quiver of the lips, and looked away, out the window—clearly to discourage further contact. He edged a bit closer to her. I couldn't see anything but their heads and shoulders except I wondered if he were bothering her in some nefarious way. Again he tried to engage her in conversation and this time she responded. Briefly. If she was being bothered or touched she could have gotten up and changed her seat, I reasoned, although she would have had to get past him, with all the clumsiness and accidental contact that would entail. She was wearing a very short skirt that was up around her smooth, tanned thighs.

Nowadays we are warned by signs on buses and subways: "If you see something, say something," a rather paltry defense against suspected terrorism, it seems to me. Even though the warning doesn't refer to suspicions of the sort I harbored, I decided to say something.

I got up and stood next to the man. "Are you bothering this young woman?" I asked. Then I addressed her directly. "Is this man bothering you?"

She looked confused and didn't answer.

He said, "I beg your pardon. I was just reminding her that we'd met before. I'm a friend of her father's. Isn't that right?" he asked, turning to her.

"Uh, yes," she said. I didn't believe her for a minute.

"Are you quite sure?" I lowered my glance to see if he was threatening her with a gun or other weapon, or, worse, if he was fumbling in his clothes. These things happen on public transportation. I didn't see any weapon or anything else untoward, which didn't mean much because he held his book bag on his lap.

"I suggest you sit elsewhere," I said to the man. "I have a feeling this young woman would prefer to sit alone." I was simply being a good citizen and trying to protect a vulnerable person; nevertheless I realized my behavior might be considered odd, even presumptuous.

"No, it's okay," she said in a wavering, high-pitched voice.

"You see?" he said to me. "Now I suggest you sit down and mind your own business."

What to do? I was almost certain that he was misbehaving, or about to misbehave. And why didn't the girl welcome my efforts to help? Had he been her age or more attractive, I could understand. But he was neither. He looked quite ordinary and when he spoke I caught a glimpse of crooked teeth. Maybe he really was a friend of her father's. Her behavior, diffident at first but slightly less so once he spoke to her, might support that claim. Still, I didn't trust him; in so short a time he had established some kind of hold over her. He might have whispered something like, "Don't move. If you do, or if you say anything, I have a gun in my pocket and I'll use it on you and all the other passengers." I am blessed, or cursed, with a powerful fantasy life and frequently imagine such scenes. I'm often proven wrong, but this time I had a strong feeling that my instincts were right.

Should I tell the driver or attempt to involve the few other passengers? No, that didn't seem likely to do much good. I'd only end up embarrassed and the object of suspicion myself.

The bus was nearing my stop. I would have to leave her unprotected, which disturbed me. But I had an appointment and couldn't wait until one of them left. Or until she called for help, which might well happen.

To ease my mind, I sought a plausible explanation for their behavior. And suddenly it dawned on me. Of course. They must be secret lovers, unlikely as it appeared. There's no accounting for taste, as the saying goes. Her mother didn't allow her to see him so they had to meet in public, innocuous places. What a relief! I could leave the bus with a clear mind.

"Don't worry," I said with a smile as I passed by. "I won't tell anyone."

They both looked up at me with puzzled faces, no doubt wondering how I had guessed their connection.

"You have such beautiful hair," I said to the girl. "You're a lucky girl, to have that hair. Take good care of it."

*   *   *

Not surprisingly, I was growing leery of public transport. I wondered why I, an unobtrusive though keenly observant person, got embroiled in distressing incidents. For instance, shortly after the day I sat behind the pretty girl with the hair, I was on another bus, not very crowded, and became aware of a high-pitched voice, faintly irritated, engaged in conversation on a cell phone. The usual thing: "I'm on the bus. I should be there in about half an hour. Where are you?"

I looked around for the source of the voice. My fellow riders were of all sorts: black, white, Asian, Latino, mostly older people, with a couple of young girls in the back whispering and giggling. (Why weren't they in school?) The voice was a woman's, a middle-aged voice that didn't fit any of the riders I saw. It gave an impression of discontent, whether with some momentary annoyance or with life in general was hard to discern. I half-rose from my seat to see if I had missed anyone, but I hadn't. In fact no one was speaking on a cell phone, which in itself is odd these days.

"Okay, call me back when you get there."

"Could it possibly be the driver? Surely drivers weren't permitted to make personal calls while driving. This driver was especially unlikely to break the rule because a Transit Authority officer was sitting near the front; he'd gotten on when I did. Moreover I was fairly sure the driver was a man, although I hadn't really paid attention when I boarded. I tried to peer over at the driver, but I couldn't see him or her from where I sat, on the left side.

"No," the woman's voice said. Still irritated; maybe she was talking to a child. Or a husband. "It's better if you call me because I'm getting off soon and I have to stop in the drugstore."

It might be a man imitating a woman's voice, though God knows why.

Again I scrutinized the passengers, one by one. Near the front next to the uniformed Transit Authority man sat a very old, thin black man with a small beard that gave him an air of distinction despite his shabby clothes. He looked frail and was sitting quietly. A young Korean woman in shorts was gazing at her phone with a smile, but not talking, probably reading a text or a Facebook post. An old white couple with shopping bags: they weren't talking at all, not even to each other, and perhaps had not for some time.

"Well, when do you think you'll get there?" the voice inquired.

A hefty woman wearing a sari, her dark hair up in a bun from which a few shiny strands had escaped, changed her seat, moving up front near the door. She wasn't on the phone, and besides, it wasn't possible that such a sharp thin voice could come out of such a soft, lardy person.

The voice had said she'd be getting off soon. I watched

the passengers leaving the bus, but no one was on the phone.

I wondered if it could be me talking. I know how strange that sounds, but because of my peculiar experiences on buses lately, I've grown suspicious of my own perceptions and behavior. But I was not planning to meet anyone or go to the drugstore, nor was I getting off soon. I had a long way to go. I wasn't even holding my phone—I checked and saw it lying quietly in my purse. Anyway, the voice didn't sound like mine.

I checked the two giggling girls at the back. Maybe they were playing some game on the phone. But no, no phone was visible.

"I'll only be at the drugstore for a few minutes. I have to pick up a prescription. Just give me about fifteen minutes, okay?"

That was the last I heard. The conversation was evidently over. No one was tucking a phone away. A seat on the right side had become vacant so I moved there in order to see the driver. It was a man, not on the phone, and besides, a bus driver wouldn't say he was getting off soon or be planning to go to the drugstore, at least not until the end of his route, and we were far from the end of the route. The driver had a long way to go, farther than I.

I was left baffled and quite unsettled. I wondered if the Transit Authority had taken to recording conversations and playing them back on the bus, to irritate the passengers, or perhaps they thought it would be diverting. But this was more than unlikely; it was mad. That I'd even thought of it increased my suspicions about my own stability.

I suppose I will never know how I came to hear the phone conversation for which I could find no rational explanation. And in the end it really doesn't matter. When I got off the bus I became preoccupied with my own affairs, and after a while I forgot about it. But the memory still returns from time to time, the vacuous conversation, the sharp somewhat impatient voice, the obvious silence of everyone on the bus except the giggling girls. The memory returns, and with it a deep unease.

* * *

The final incident occurred on a subway. The train had stopped several times between stations, in the dark, deep underground. Each stop lasted a long time. The passengers were showing signs of impatience, scowls, head shaking, muttering. This latest time, the lights flickered on and off. People looked around with puzzled glances, as if someone could explain what was happening. A baby was yelling its head off at the far end of the car. Panic began seeping in through the closed windows, as it does whenever a train stops in the dark for a long time. The homeless man sprawled on the double seat in the corner snored and smelled bad. Before, when the train was in motion, an empty beer bottle at his feet rolled back and forth, making a clinking noise every time it hit the metal pole, but now the bottle was at rest.

"We are being delayed because of subway traffic ahead," came a familiar sharp male baritone we had heard on the previous stops. Mr. Subway Computer's voice. "We will be moving shortly. We are sorry for any inconvenience." How could a computer voice feel sorry? The offense of it! The sheer nerve, offering us Mr. Subway Computer's recorded apologies! I seethed. I got hot all over. It was a good thing the air-conditioning was working. Otherwise everyone would get hot and there might be a riot.

A human voice broke in, harsh and cracked with static: "The number 1 local train will be running on the express track. The number 2 train will not be running. The number 3 train will make its last stop at 96th Street. If you want to continue further, go upstairs and take a shuttle bus." There was more but I covered my ears. I was dizzy. I might faint. I gazed around to see if there was anyone who might revive me when I fainted. No one looked likely. I was the oldest person in the car. Why should they care if I fainted?

"Because of a police investigation no trains will stop at 23rd and 28th Street . . ." Mr. Subway Computer Voice said. That, I knew because I had read about it in the paper, was because of the terrorist attack, the explosion, yesterday. Maybe another terrorist attack was going on at the very next station. We would all be killed—and not in a very nice way—and it would be bad for our country. But at least this waiting in the dark would be over. And the announcements would stop.

The endless delays and the announcements over the loudspeaker in the staticky voice and the screaming baby jostled in my head like an aggressive avant-garde symphony. Maybe that baby knew something the rest of us didn't. The homeless man's smell wafted through the car. The faces of my fellow passengers spun around. Any minute someone would lose control and scream. Chaos would erupt. That person might very well be me. I felt the scream in the pit of my stomach, slowly rising. I even looked forward to it, to the moment when it would rise through my chest and break free from my throat. What a release it would be, to lose control and scream in a full subway car. What would happen? They would come for me with a straitjacket and carry me away. Good. As long as it was quiet wherever they took me. And above ground: light and air.

Mr. Subway Computer Voice said, "If you see something, say something." I looked around to see what I could see. Nothing but the other passengers. All of them—black, white, male, female, young, old—looked sinister. Their mouths drooped. Which of them were carrying guns? The younger ones, most likely. Which of them was likely to lose patience and pull out the gun? (If I had a gun, I'd pull it out.) Not the boy with the earphones, leaning on the door, jiggling in time to his music—he was somewhere else. Maybe the one fussing with his hair across from me. He fussed and fussed with his voluminous hair, arranging and rearranging it on the top of his head, then put on a wool hat. It was hot out, why would he wear a wool hat?

Mr. Subway Computer Voice said, "Assaulting a subway employee is a felony punishable by up to seven years in prison." No subway employees were in sight. And we were imprisoned already.

I could yell, Get that screaming baby out of here! But there was nowhere to go. The doors were locked. Beyond them were the darkness and the tracks. Blood stomped through my neck. The scream was ascending, brushing past my rib cage.

The automated voice said, "Please keep track of your property. Do not display cell phones or other electronic equipment." Next to the man with the wool hat, three young women in short skirts, their six thighs lined up like logs on a raft, were playing with their phones. One woman at the far end of the row was calmly reading a book. If only I had a book. Why hadn't I brought a book? I could snatch her book away and start reading it, I wouldn't care what it was. This was no time to be fussy. But I was too weak to stand—my legs were shaking.

The train moved. The sinister faces relaxed with relief. We slid slowly into a station. People got off and others took their place, new, innocent people. They didn't know what we had been through. The screaming baby didn't get off. A man in a black metal helmet pushed his way in with a bicycle and people glared at him.

The train slid slowly out of the station and again stopped in the dark for a long time. The staticky cracked voice came back: "There is another train ahead of us. We will be moving shortly." The voice repeated the message about the numbers 1, 2, and 3 trains and the shuttle buses waiting upstairs on the street. I wiped my sweaty face with a tissue and hid my face in my hands.

My scream was almost ready to break free. But it would be a deliberate scream, not a losing-control scream. I could still control it. I pondered the difference between losing control and consciously letting the impatient scream in my throat burst out. It was a subtle difference, hard to pinpoint. I've always suspected there is an element of purposefulness in madness. The mad know what they are doing. They could control themselves; they just don't choose to any longer. Is that the same as losing control? I knew I was about to scream any minute and didn't try to restrain it. I wanted the pleasure of release.

"If you see any suspicious activity, don't keep it to yourself. Tell a subway employee."

I screamed, loud and long. Just opened my mouth and let it out. It felt good, as I expected. It drowned out the screaming of the baby. The baby couldn't control herself, but I could. I just didn't care to make the effort anymore. A few people gathered around me, either to help me or shut me up, but I covered my face with my hands to keep them away. The computer voice came on again, "If you see something, say something." How could I see with my hands over my face?

I screamed until the train pulled into a station. There

were three people in uniform waiting at the door. I staggered out and they took my arms.

"I couldn't help it," I said. But that wasn't true. I just didn't want to control myself anymore.

Tree of Porphyry

"I try to give my dog the chance to be a dog whenever I can."
The speaker was a hefty gray-haired man with avia-
tor-style glasses, wearing a parka—one might say packed
into a parka. He was addressing a woman standing near
him. On this city street with a fair number of walkers, some
accompanied by dogs, even a professional dog walker with
his little herd, it was unclear whether the woman the hefty
man spoke to was a companion or a stranger. She was about
his age, fifty-five or so, and was tugging her dog—or a dog,
not to assume too much; it might have been a neighbor's
and she was helping out—anyway, trying to tug a large
woolly honey-colored dog away from the clump of leaves
and dirt it was burrowing in at the base of a tree.

The man's remark was curious, raising the question of
what being a dog entails, or suggesting there are circumstances in which a dog would not be a dog. He apparently
felt it his duty towards dogs and their essence to correct the
woman for not letting the dog rummage freely. That is what
being a dog means, after all, or rather one of the many things
being a dog means. As if to demonstrate, the dog struggled
to keep nosing at the base of the tree. A common city tree,
linden, maple, or ginkgo.

Definitely not a tree of Porphyry, which is not a tangible tree of any interest to dogs but an ancient design illus-

trating a logical progression, devised by the third-century Greek philosopher Porphyry, and derived from Aristotle's chart of categories of everything in the world.

Porphyry's tree, familiar (though not by that name) to readers of hypertext fiction or creators of algorithms, is used to parse categories such as animal, vegetable, mineral, and whatever else. The trunk divides into two branches, one on either side, which divide into two more branches, and each of those four branches divides into two more, and so on and so on until all varieties of the topic being investigated are exhausted, if ever.

But where, meanwhile, was the man's alluded-to dog? Left at home, it seems, missing out on the opportunity to be a dog and burrow. Or more accurately, the opportunity to behave like a dog. There is a distinction between being and behaving, one essential and the other contingent, to borrow from Aristotle. Dogs behaving unlike dogs is possible if uncommon. As for being, what else could a dog be? Was the man intimating that the woman was treating the dog like a person, say, a child (perhaps fondly recalling a child of her own), who most people would agree should not stick his or her nose into a pile of leaves, twigs, stones, and dirt? Yet the woman's dog, or at any rate the dog she tugged, was indeed behaving like a dog by struggling to remain at the tree. So there is really no way to prevent a dog from being a dog, and anyway, why would you?

Maybe the woman had a reason, other than misguided discipline or plain ignorance of what dogs are like, for tugging the dog away from the underbrush. Maybe the dog had recently had some illness that made it inadvisable to burrow in dirt, or maybe it had once choked on a twig and she feared its happening again, particularly if this were not her dog and she was helping out a sick or otherwise occupied neighbor. It would be calamitous to return a dog that was choking or had expired from choking on a twig, if dogs eat twigs—if that is part of being a dog, though I suspect not. It would be even worse had the dog been put in her charge for a period of time longer than a walk, say a week, by a friend or cousin or lover who trusted her enough despite her ignorance about dogs being dogs.

If, as is more likely, the dog belonged to the woman, it might have been a brand-new dog and she was being especially careful, never having owned a dog before. If she was divorced or widowed she might have gotten the dog for company, to relieve the loneliness that overcame her in the early morning hours, the empty left side of the bed, or in the evening the silent spaces where every creak promised a footstep that never came. Or if her husband was incommunicative or surly or away on frequent business trips, or, sadly, too transformed by illness to be the true companion he once was. Or she might have acquired the dog to allay or distract her from some grief—the death of a loved one (the adored mother who at the end regarded her with a cold, impassive eye), or being abandoned by a lover, or a very serious professional setback that put her entire future in peril. Or she missed her children who were grown and gone, gone so far off to alien climates and time zones that they might as well have been on the moon; missed them in their youth when they pattered and clattered and scattered around the house. But a dog is not a good substitute for a child precisely because it is a dog and behaves like one. It does not learn to talk or go to school or ride a bike. That is what children do, behaving like the children they are for so brief a time.

As a matter of fact, children, in their play, often behave like dogs or cats or elephants or birds, but while these imitations can be carried to absurd reaches of imagination, never do the children become or truly try to become those creatures except in cases of psychological aberration. (Believing they can fly, for example, with tragic results.)

The man, for his part, behaving like the man he was, might well have had a motive more pointed than guidance in dog rearing. He might have found her attractive, with her mass of curly gray hair, her slim figure in tight jeans and tan suede boots and a fringed scarf over her shoulders, plus her colorful tote bag that suggested a Latin American country where people still wove such bags (was she an intrepid traveler? he wondered, though chances are the bag came from a catalogue devoted to products by native craftspeople). His curiosity was aroused as he approached the half-hearted urban tree (linden or ginkgo or maple or whatever, but certainly not the abstract tree of Porphyry), where she tugged at the leash with difficulty, because the dog was heavy and stubbornly fixed on behaving like a dog, having no alternative.

The man looked cheery, pleased with himself, but not irritatingly so; his pleasure seemed to include the world around him, as if he had just heard good news he wanted to share, as if at any moment he might begin to skip or leap into the air. He decided on the spot to strike up a conversation in the hopes of forming a connection, or at least to determine whether he would want a connection, depending on her response and demeanor. If so, that is to his credit, since many men his age would have passed her by unnoticed, preferring women fifteen or twenty years younger.

What better way to begin an acquaintance than to allude to a common interest such as dogs, their behavior and care? With this end in mind, he must have realized it would have been useful to be accompanied by his own dog. Quite a few loving couples can trace their origin to a dog-walking encounter. But as it happened, he had walked his dog earlier that day—how could he have foreseen the need for its company later? Moreover, he was coming from a doctor's office, where dogs being dogs are definitely not welcome, and where he was relieved to learn he was in excellent health. Which news might have made him all the more eager to meet an attractive woman, particularly if not long ago he had suffered the loss of his beloved terminally ill wife, a loss he carried like a weight on his heart yet not incompatible with noticing women on the street. Or he had been divorced: a tedious, soul-destroying saga which, if he formed any kind of connection with the attractive woman, he would doubtless recount to her at length.

As soon as the words were out of his mouth surely he grasped—unless his social awareness was undeveloped—that an implied or overt criticism was not the best way to strike up an acquaintance. But it was too late. On the other hand perhaps the woman was not sensitive to criticism about her treatment of dogs—indeed could laugh it off and find his ill-considered remark amusing, certainly enough to initiate a conversation, even an acquaintanceship.

Unless we broaden the ramifications of this encounter, move on to a different branch of the abstract tree, it could devolve into a romantic comedy, a meeting-cute story. Not to denigrate that genre, of which there are many charming examples, yet it would cut off more fruitful branches of our inquiry. For instance, instead of focusing on canine care and leading to an invitation for coffee in the nearby café, the story might take a philosophical turn, such as: What is being a dog (and, by extension, a person)? Need a dog be "given a chance" to be a dog? Or is it not presumptuous of its owner to assume a dog requires permission to be a dog when it so obviously is one already, any more than a person requires permission to be a person, although there are many instances in which people are denied their rights to full personhood and the pursuit of their destiny as persons. You can read about them in the papers every day.

The word "owner" itself is questionable: can one creature ever "own" another? (Ownership inevitably raises the issue of slavery, a subject so freighted with historical, social, and psychological baggage for both victims and perpetrators that it warrants far more serious treatment than a frivolous study such as this one can manage; fortunately historians and scholars have treated it in depth.) Dogs and other animals are casually bought and sold in stores along with inanimate objects and no one protests; certainly not the animals, being what they are.

A dog is called man's best friend, but since when did friends ever own each other? Granted, some friendships do involve disparities in power and position that undermine the ideal of friendship as a relation between equals. But in no case can ownership be involved. (In certain cultures and historical periods, a man was or is considered to own his wife, maybe even his children. However, in the social context of this man and this woman on the street near the drooping tree, any ensuing connection would not involve ownership—unless one of the parties proved mad or obsessive.)

We have proceeded on the assumption that the man and woman were strangers. But—to leap back to an earlier branch, with apologies to Porphyry—the man's remark would generate different ramifications if the pair were not strangers, if they had already formed one of the infinite degrees of connection. That they were not married or cohabiting lovers we can safely posit, for in those cases the man would already have made known his views on the treatment of burrowing dogs. They could be potential lovers, people who had gone out on the occasional date but not yet embarked on intimacy, perhaps because maturity had made them wary. In that case, his remark during a casual dog walk together might be part of the ritual and often tedious getting-to-know-you process, confiding one's habits, histories, and predilections. Unless, on the contrary, maturity had hastened intimacy, with the awareness of fleeting time.

They might have recognized each other through proximity, meeting here and there in the neighborhood. Maybe their children had attended the same primary school but they hadn't seen each other in the years since PTA meetings. Or the woman worked in a local shop the man frequented, the kind of slim connection that would make it rude to walk by without at least a cursory greeting (though not requiring a critical comment). Or he had been the principal of her son's high school where they had had a few tense meetings regarding the boy's misbehavior, let us hope for her sake nothing serious like drugs or theft, just mild disobedience or drawing graffiti on the walls near the lockers—the same mischievous boy who would come home covered with mud or splinters after exploring some deep puddle or rotting fence and who now lived at the ends of the earth where who knows what he might be up to.

They might have run into each other at a local gym (each appeared to be in good shape, as far as a glance could reveal), or belong to a political club or amateur chamber music group. He would play the viola and she the soulful cello, and they shared the sort of intimacy that evolves in such groups (or amateur theater groups or Tai Chi classes) as over time each member learns the others' abilities and tendencies while knowing next to nothing of their private lives. (He had already noticed her with interest, but as a loving husband, he was preoccupied with caring for his terminally ill wife.) If so, this chance encounter on the street would place them in an unfamiliar setting, forcing them to revise—with unease and/or surprise—their earlier impressions. Let us hope they hadn't met at a therapy group, as that could cause extreme discomfort, not because each knew little of the other's personal life, but too much and not flattering. The same would apply to AA meetings.

A casual acquaintance of this kind could account for the awkward or sententious nature of the man's remark on dogs and their existential destiny. Yet even so, the scenario might lead to coffee in the nearby café, neither one at the moment seeking a romantic companion—each maybe having a satisfactory mate at home whose name or existence ("my wife," "my husband") they might let drop in an offhand way so as to prevent misunderstanding of their intentions—simply a friendly sit-down in which the man would apologize for his impromptu criticism and the woman could brush it off as insignificant, or praise it as witty (even if unintentionally so). Each would find out what the other did when not attending the chamber group (Tai Chi class, et al.). A lawyer, an accountant, a yoga teacher, a website designer, a building contractor, a jewelry importer, an ICU nurse, a dressmaker (more likely her), a computer repairman, a corporate executive (more likely him), a proofreader . . . When they got home they could say to their respective mates, You'll never guess who I ran into on the street, this guy (woman) from my chamber group (political club, gym) and we had coffee. She/he is very interesting, I never realized because we usually just talk about the music (candidates, exercise equipment . . .).

The foregoing is a mere sample of the possibilities surrounding this chance encounter, which though not infinite are vast. We've barely begun on a tree that could reach the heavens. Not to mention the broader questions of ownership, the existential nature of living creatures and how far that nature might be altered or circumvented. That is, can any creature be or behave like something other than what it is? Scientific studies have induced animals to go beyond their customary behavior, witness experiments in teaching chimps to understand or use language. These generally have limited success, never reaching the higher levels of nuanced language. What they prove is that an ability to use or understand very simple language is part of what being a chimp is, and needs only strenuous efforts, of uncertain value, to be elicited. Mice or rats trained to push buttons for food or react with fear to certain stimuli do not so much elucidate the nature of rodents as help to predict or, more sinisterly, control the behavior of human beings. In short, the evidence suggests that, in the words of the old saying, boys will be boys.

The range of possibilities for our couple would multiply further if we mixed them up—like throwing scraps of paper into the air and seeing where they land—yielding new permutations. For instance, it could be the man who had a surly and uncommunicative wife at home, which is why he craved sympathetic companionship, while the woman was recently and unhappily divorced, although should coffee in the nearby café lead to further involvement, she would be less likely to recount her saga in excruciating detail. Or she was the high-school principal and he the father of the problem child, a girl refusing to conform to the dress code of dull chinos and T-shirt, preferring miniskirts, and who kept her contrariness to this day, with a reputation as a political activist that brought him both pride and dismay. Or he was the one who suffered the serious professional setback, even lost his position unjustly, leading to the alarming symptoms that drove him to the doctor's office where he learned that the symptoms were due to stress rather than to a serious illness.

As for their future, who can say? If strangers, they might simply walk on, though despite his disapproval, the man, out of chivalry, would help her get the recalcitrant dog away from the tree. Or else proceed warily to the coffee shop and the wide-open future with its array of outcomes. If acquaintances, the same coffee shop, altering the nature of their acquaintance a jot, so that the next time they met at the political club they might find seats together. Or more than a jot. There is just so much that one can speculate after overhearing an unusual remark on the street, just so far one is willing to travel down endlessly bifurcating paths.

But before leaving our trees, real and abstract, a final word about the lurking subtextual question. Dogs, we have established, can be nothing but dogs. Can humans behave or be other than human? Victims of torture can be made to do things not in their individual natures, such as betraying allies or confessing to crimes they did not commit. But they do not thereby cease to be or behave like persons: such behavior, while constrained and regrettable, is within the bounds of human nature. Likewise with slaves, indentured servants, women forced into prostitution, whose unwilling acts are also within that range. Can a person behave so far beyond accepted human behavior that he or she can be considered no longer human and undeserving of being treated as such? Unfortunately, the range of human behavior is so broad that one can barely imagine what might go beyond it. We can and do readily label some behaviors "inhumane."

But "inhuman," though a shorter word, goes farther. Can anyone behave so badly as to merit ejection from Aristotle's category "human"? Some certainly try.

Apples

As an infant, she was what mothers call a good eater. She took breast milk, she accepted solid food at a few months, and she thrived. By the time she was four, she could speak quite cogently and enjoyed being read to and looking at picture books. She shared her mother's love of music, and whenever music was playing she would prance around the house as lively children do. She appeared to be progressing well.

But around the time she learned to run and skip, something changed. She became indifferent to food. She ate as before, but without enthusiasm, and seemed to have no preferences and no interest in new tastes. She was not a hunger artist like the character in Kafka's famous story, who claimed he abjured food because he had never found a food he liked, and eventually grew scrawny and died. Not at all: the girl ate what she was given, but out of obedience or habit, apparently, rather than desire. She didn't jump for joy like most children when offered treats like ice cream or cookies. She accepted them as if they were no different from the usual daily fare. Unlike adolescents with eating disorders, she was too young to be obsessed by her weight or appearance and was hardly fixated on food—on the contrary, she was indifferent.

She went to school and did the things children do, yet

a kind of apathy seeped through her, as though the apathy about food had spread throughout her being. She felt an obscure lack, as of something needed but as yet undiscovered. Her worried mother took her to doctors to see if her taste buds were deficient, or if she harbored a serious disease, but she was always found to be in good health.

Then at around age nine or ten, another change occurred. Her mother, always in search of something to whet her daughter's appetite, had discovered a new kind of apple at the farmers' market. Naturally the girl had eaten apples before. Her mother had tried every variety of fruit and vegetable. As is well known, there are dozens of kinds of apples. Besides the common McIntosh, Granny Smith, and Delicious, there are the lesser known and beautifully named, such as Pink Lady, Fuji, Ginger Gold, Ambrosia, Liberty, Lady Alice, not to mention those plucked by Yeats's Wandering Aengus, "the silver apples of the moon, the golden apples of the sun."

This new apple, bright red with yellow and amber streaks, whose name no one at the market could or would supply, proved a success. The child came alive at the first bite. Her eyes opened wide and she beamed with pleasure. "This is so good!" she cried.

Her mother was naturally delighted, and from then on bought quantities of the special apple. The girl would eat several at once. Her mother warned that so many apples could make her sick, but they never did make her sick. They brought forth her good spirits, making her elated and energetic and enthusiastic. She was a changed girl. Though never before given to supernatural thinking, her mother wondered if there might be something magical about them. But when she timidly suggested this to the pediatrician, a man of science, he laughed and said they were one of Mother Nature's gifts; she mustn't let her imagination run away with her.

One day, after seeing a production of *The Sleeping Beauty* on television, the girl announced that she wanted to take ballet classes. She had never mentioned that before, although she had always pranced around the house to music and had danced in little school productions. Her mother thought it a whim but saw no reason not to indulge it. A visiting dancer friend had once remarked on the supple ease of the girl's movements and said she had the perfect dancer's body. Provided, that is, it didn't change with puberty, which unfortunately happens with many little girls who dream of being dancers, of playing princesses and sylphs, only to find themselves, at around twelve or thirteen, transformed by breasts and hips that defy the requirements of classical ballet.

The girl began attending classes at the school of a distinguished ballet company where she quickly stood out. She worked hard, she went to class every day, and by the time she was a teenager, having kept her perfect dancer's body, was given roles in the corps de ballet. And after a few more years, solo roles. While her fellow ballerinas struggled to maintain the punishing standards of thinness their art demanded, for her, with her indifference to food, there was no difficulty. Of course she kept an ample supply of the special apples. Her mother was relieved that the girl had found a calling she loved and did well.

She was passionate about her work and wanted nothing else. She danced her way into early middle age and even beyond, but inevitably the time came, as with all ballerinas, when her body could no longer do what the arduous roles demanded. Or rather, her body could execute the movements, but with greater and greater effort, and with less of the ease that had been her distinctive quality. She wasn't heartbroken, she knew this would happen; she was grateful for all the years she had had. Like many older dancers, she became a ballet mistress and coached young dancers, which she could expect to do for a good while. The world of dance would still be her world.

What did threaten her equanimity, though, a year or so after she began coaching, was a shortage of the apples she relied on. For reasons she couldn't fathom, perhaps having to do with agricultural production or globalization or climate change, the special apples, whose provenance she had never learned, were no longer widely available. She had to search the stores for them, sometimes to no avail. Without them, the old apathy of her early childhood began seeping into her.

Since she was used to eating very little besides the apples, she grew thinner. On the advice of the company's physician she forced herself to return to the normal diet that long ago she had found so dull and tasteless. She obeyed; she knew his advice was sensible. But she mourned for the apples as she might have for a loved one. She was heartsick without the buoyancy she had come to take for granted, and sickened by her own apathy. Without the stage, without the apples, her life felt drab, drained of ardor, as it had before the apples, before the dancing.

But her training had instilled the habit of discipline and she carried on with her work, occasionally stirred when she discovered a young dancer of potential brilliance, or managed to elicit an instant of perfection from her students. She felt both pleasure and rue at those moments, elated by the young ones who performed feats she could now only demonstrate sketchily.

She continued to hunt for the apples, and now and then

she did find a few, which she hastily grabbed from the bin. And when she ate them she indeed felt the old eagerness and energy returning. At times she could even leap across the room as she used to, while her students watched in awe. She understood very well that it wasn't the apples that gave her the ability to dance. That was inborn, and honed by years of practice. What the apples gave her was the will and the aspiration.

There came a time when the apples were once more widely available. Something must have changed in the global marketplace. She was old now, old, at least, for a dancer. When she ate them, on occasion she could summon a trace of her former fluidity of movement. But the apples seemed to be losing their power to animate her. At first she thought the fruit itself might be different; maybe the crops had failed or the farmers had adopted different methods. When she asked at the markets, she was assured that they were the same apples as ever. But for her they were not the same, and so she was not the same.

Finally the old apathy overcame her desire for the apples. She liked bringing them home, liked looking at them in a bowl on her kitchen table, the same tantalizing bright red streaked with yellow and amber. They reminded her of her best days, when her gift had unfurled effortlessly. But she didn't eat them.

Sometimes she urged herself, just try one! But something stubborn in her refused to court disappointment. Almost certainly they would not work the magic they used to work. She pined for what they had once given. But picking one up and eating it took courage—a courage only they could give—and she was tired. The tasteless foods she ate out of obligation and habit, as in her childhood, would have to do, as they did for so many others.

An Impromptu Visit

The windshield wipers were going full speed, as if fleeing from danger. But the rain was coming down so hard that the windows were sheeted with water between each swipe. My daughter, beside me in the death seat, kept wiping the inside of the front window with an old rag she found under the seat but it fogged up immediately because I couldn't figure out which was the defrost button. There was no way we could go on like this, I was too rattled and the rain was too heavy, so I pulled slowly over onto the shoulder, dreading a skid. We both felt better once we stopped, but that wasn't very safe either since the shoulders on the Parkway are narrow and we might be near an exit or entry ramp; I couldn't tell in the rain.

"What'll we do?" she asked. I wished she could take over the driving—she has a steadier nature than I—but like most city kids her age, seventeen, she hadn't yet learned to drive.

"We'll sit here awhile until it lets up."

But it didn't let up. We waited about fifteen minutes and she said, "Let's try again. We could be here for hours."

I eased into traffic, but the car moved in syncopated lurches, slowing then speeding up, like it was doing a dance.

"There's something wrong with the car," I said. "I'm getting off at the next exit." I wasn't the greatest driver in the world, but I hadn't yet had an accident with Lucy in the car with me, and I wanted to keep it that way.

"But we're in the middle of nowhere."

"It's not nowhere. It's the Palisades. We're in suburban New Jersey. We'll find something."

I took the next exit ramp, which was thankfully soon. Right away I spotted a post office (closed, it was Sunday) so I turned into their almost empty parking lot. "Well, this is lucky. I can't drive this old thing anymore. We'll call Ron." I knew about the AAA but I preferred Ron. "Ron to the rescue," I said in an attempt to lighten the mood in the car, but Lucy didn't respond.

He was my big brother, ten years older. We'd just come from visiting him about twenty miles north. He wouldn't be happy about rescuing us but he'd do it. It would hardly be the first time he'd gotten me out of a tough situation, starting in high school when I took a boy's copy of *The Call of the Wild*. I'm not sure what made me do it, but it had a great picture of a dog on the cover and I was lured by the title. Ron replaced it so I didn't have to tell my parents, who would have had a fit. Most recently he came through again when my marriage fell apart and I needed a protection order. Ron was reliable and looked out for me. He was also a car expert, born to drive. He'd been driving since the age of thirteen, when my father taught him in deserted parking lots like the one we were in. It was one of the few interests and talents they shared.

I dug my phone out of my purse but it wouldn't work. Of course—I'd forgotten to charge it overnight and meant to do it at Ron's house, where we'd spent the afternoon swimming in his pool and sunning ourselves on deck chairs.

When it came to phones, Lucy could be counted on. "Mine is dead," I said. "You try."

She didn't quite roll her eyes but I could feel the adolescent scorn like a faint shadow passing over me.

"Shit," she said. "I can't get a signal. It must be the weather. Or this nowhere place." She kept trying, then gave up.

I took a deep breath. "Well, we'll just have to knock on someone's door and ask to use their phone."

"Lots of luck," she said. "If this was Texas they'd shoot us, but here they'll just slam the door in our face."

"We have no choice. Come on."

We had no umbrellas or jackets. Rain hadn't been expected until late at night. The minute we got out of the car we were soaked. But very soon we found ourselves on a suburban street lined with houses. We ran up the walk of the nearest one, a neat ranch with drooping violets on the front lawn. I rang the bell and a middle-aged woman with dark curly hair, wearing baggy jeans and a man's shirt, came to the door. She looked alarmed.

"I'm so sorry to bother you," I began. "Our car broke down on the highway. Our phones aren't working so I wonder if I might use your phone to ask my brother to pick us up. He lives just a few miles away." This was a slight exaggeration—it was about twenty miles.

She clearly didn't know what to do. The story sounded reasonable enough, and we didn't look like serial killers or thieves, whatever thieves look like—just a wet woman a bit younger than herself and a teenager in shorts with a backpack. I could read her mind: They look innocent enough but you can never tell. For example, what's in the backpack? (Bathing suits and towels, but she couldn't know that.) On the other hand, could she turn us away in the storm? She must have been alone in the house. Otherwise she would have called out to someone and been relieved of making the decision.

It didn't occur to me to be frightened. After all, I might

have stumbled upon a den of dangerous criminals or a psychopath eagerly waiting for victims—it would be just my luck. But I was too wet and desperate to think past getting out of the rain.

"Okay," the woman said finally, good nature winning out. "Come in. Wipe your feet on the mat, please."

"Thank you so much," we said with relief that surely appeared genuine.

The first room we entered was the kitchen, a large brightly lit room with gleaming white appliances, everything neat and clean, a teapot on the stove.

"Let me get you some towels to dry your hair," she said.

When she disappeared for a moment we looked around. There were kids' drawings held on the refrigerator with magnets, a poster of a bowl of peaches, probably Cézanne, and on a windowsill an avocado pit in a glass of water with toothpicks. I had grown avocado plants in the same way. She returned with towels and led me to the phone in the hall.

"What's the address?" I asked. "I don't even know what town we're in. I couldn't read the signs." She told me what exit Ron should take, and wrote down her address on a scrap of paper she handed to me.

Ron gave a slight groan but said okay, as I knew he would. He'd start out right away. I gave him the address. "And take it easy," I said. "It's an awful storm."

Hearing my rather confused directions about finding the house, the woman said, "I'd better talk to him." So I passed her the phone and she explained everything clearly. She gave him her number in case he got lost on the way. When she hung up she even offered to call a local service station about my car but I said not to bother, Ron would deal with it.

We returned to the kitchen, where my daughter was fluffing out her damp hair.

"Thank you so much," I said. "This is so kind of you. Come on, Lucy, we'll wait in the car. Ron'll be here in a little while."

"Oh no," the woman said. "I can't let you wait in the car in this weather." Her fear had ebbed; if we had mayhem in mind, we would have begun already. Now that help was on the way, I relaxed and felt surprise at how trusting she was of total strangers. What made this nice woman so sure we weren't thieves or serial killers? Of course we weren't, but still . . . She wasn't even alarmed that a strange man would be arriving, perhaps to assist us in some nefarious crime.

So we settled in to wait, and the woman made us tea. She put out a plate of pecan sandies, my favorite cookie. We had lucked out.

She told us about her house. She and her husband had lived there for over twenty years and raised their two sons, who were away at college. Her husband was off on a business trip but would be back that evening, unless his plane was delayed by the storm. He was in the window-treatment business—drapes, curtains, shades. She offered to show us her living room. As I might have expected, there were fashionable translucent shades on the windows, through which the raindrops glinted like gems, as well as wine-colored draperies. The room was arranged for comfort: a couch and matching easy chairs, an Oriental rug, a large TV, and several end tables that held some ivory figurines they had purchased on a trip to Japan. She was very proud of these and rightly so. They were delicately made, exquisite: an elephant, a samurai warrior, a reclining woman, maybe a geisha. The best was a little Buddha, about four inches high, with a big belly and bare feet. He appeared to be smiling slyly.

Back in the kitchen, we drank our tea and chatted away about children and colleges. Our hostess was quite comfortable now, far more so than I would have been in her position. Experiences in the city have made me wary of strangers. But she seemed almost glad of the company. Lucy, too, became quite talkative. When asked about school she volunteered that she would be starting her senior year and applying to colleges, which led our hostess to recall the times when her sons were applying—they were fortunate to be accepted at their first choices. I ate two pecan sandies. In addition to being grateful, I liked her. She was a generous soul.

It was growing darker now outside the kitchen window. My brother should be arriving any minute. And indeed the bell rang just as I had this thought, a curious concordance, as if my thought had caused him to appear at the door. I'd always been proud of my brother, so successful and competent at everything, while I was the scattered and disorganized one, still going from job to job, still counting on him to get me out of trouble. I was newly impressed that he had located the place without needing to phone for help.

Ron entered, wearing a slicker and a rain hat, and introduced himself. The woman offered him a towel but he declined. He barely looked at me and I could see he was impatient to get going. He had to get us to the city, then drive all the way back home. When we got in the car he would surely ask me how on earth I had gotten into this predicament, a question he had had reason to ask on several previous occasions. I was not looking forward to that.

Before we left I asked if I could use the bathroom and our hostess pointed it out. The way back took me through the living room, where I slipped the tiny Buddha into my jeans pocket. I pulled my shirt down so Lucy wouldn't notice the bulge. I didn't want to set a bad example, have her think we were the kind of people who would do such things. We weren't. It was a sudden impulse, irresistible. I've had those urges before, often in crowded department stores, but I always managed to fight them off. I knew right from wrong. I would send the little Buddha back tomorrow. I'd wrap it carefully in bubble wrap since it was so delicate, and mail it in the morning.

Even now I can't say precisely why I did that. I do things sometimes and don't understand why. With the Buddha it was as if something primitive sparked up in me from a pre-historic time when people simply grabbed what they want-ed. A time before there was a moral code. But was there ever such a time? No, I bet even primitive people had an inkling of the difference between mine and not-mine.

Maybe I felt I deserved a reward for the stress of driving in the rain and not getting us killed, for handling the situ-ation sensibly. I often feel I deserve better than I've gotten. Or it might have been a warning to our hostess, that she shouldn't trust strangers so readily. Who knows, the next time a stranger knocked on her door it might well be a seri-al killer or a thief. Besides, I really liked the little figure, so plump and cheerful. I was like a child spying a shiny object glinting in the grass. I wanted it to be mine. At least for a while.

The nice woman would be dismayed when she found the Buddha gone, which was too bad. She would regret her kindness, the tea, the pecan sandies, and would lose faith in her instincts and her judgments of people, which in our case had been correct. Our story was true and we didn't pose a physical threat. When she received the Buddha back, she would be grateful, as if it were a gift, which it certainly was not: it belonged to her. Still, she would appreciate the gesture, even in her bafflement.

Lucy and I were glad to settle in at home and put on dry clothes. I gave Ron the car keys and told him exactly where the car was parked, in the post office lot just off the exit ramp, and he said he'd take care of it in the morning. We thanked him profusely—I always did—but he wouldn't even stay for a drink or a cup of tea. I had cookies too, not pecan sandies but dull oatmeal raisin. Why not wait until the rain let up, I urged, I'd order a pizza? But he left in a hurry. I did order a pizza and Lucy and I watched TV for a while, then we went to bed early. I could hear her on the phone in her room, telling her best friend about our adventure. I hid the ivory Buddha in a dresser drawer, wrapped in a nightgown.

The next morning I packed it carefully in bubble wrap and found a small box just the right size to mail it back in. But I couldn't find the scrap of paper where the woman had written her address. Where could I have put it? I checked the pockets of my still damp jeans and emptied my purse, but nothing. This was extremely distressing, not at all what I intended. I couldn't ask Lucy, and she wouldn't have the scrap of paper anyway. Reluctantly, I called Ron. Maybe he'd written down the address or would remember it. I told him I wanted to write a thank you note—a good idea, in fact. I might do just that. But no such luck. Knowing Ron, I was sure he could easily find his way back there and get the address, but he didn't suggest that and I couldn't, just for a thank you note. That would be asking too much. Also, I realized I didn't even know the woman's name. With all our conviviality, we hadn't gotten around to names. Could you mail a package to an address without a name? Probably, on a street like that. But at this point the whole thing was too involved, her husband would be back, she'd have to explain . . . "They seemed so nice," she'd say. Once again, my impulses had gotten me into a situation with unintended consequences, as they say about wars.

Before we hung up Ron said, "I'll call my service station now and have them get your car."

The car. I'd forgotten about it. I hoped it was beyond repair. If they fixed it, I'd have to go up there by bus to bring it back. Not to mention the expense of repairs.

"Thanks," I murmured. "For everything."

"Righto," he said, and was gone.

I still have the little Buddha in the dresser drawer. I couldn't put it out on a table because of Lucy. She got into her first-choice college, by the way—like the woman's sons—and with a scholarship and some help from Ron she was able to attend. Even with her away, I can't bring myself to take it out of the drawer. Just touching it, wrapped in the nightgown, makes me feel so awful. So ashamed. And as baffled as my victim.

A Few Days Off

A certain woman woke up one day feeling very tired. Burnt out, as they call it, as if the flame of energy had waned and finally succumbed to the ambient air currents. She had been working hard, the weather was gray and heavy, and perhaps, she thought, she was getting a touch of flu. She would spend a couple of days in bed. There would be no great harm done at work. She was director of Human Services, hiring and firing; a number of major shifts in staff had just taken place, and things were quieter. If anything came up, her capable assistant could take care of it.

She called in sick (rare for her), settled into bed with a cup of tea and a few magazines, and felt quite contented. After dozing on and off for a while, she discovered it was late afternoon and got up to make herself a sandwich. She turned off her phone, just in case. It was surprising how peaceful it felt, cocooned in bed, sliding in and out of sleep, thinking of nothing in particular.

In the evening she watched some television, read a bit, and ate another sandwich. She spent the following day the same way. The time passed pleasantly, and she didn't relish getting up to go to work the next day. Her calendar showed she had two interviews scheduled, for low-level staff. Her assistant could easily handle those.

She called in sick again, saying she had the flu and might be out for several more days, and instructed her assistant to do the scheduled interviews; her assistant reported nothing of moment and hoped she'd feel better soon. Anything I can get you? she asked. No thanks, that's kind of you, but I have all I need and everyone delivers anyway. If I'm not back by Monday check up on the new hires in Administration and see how things are going.

Gazing at the phone brought the familiar tug of responsibility, and so with reluctance she checked her email and texts. Nothing of importance: political announcements and petitions, a reminder of a dental appointment the following morning, two friends, one of whom wanted someone's email address, and a text from a man she'd recently met reminding her of their date in a few days. She texted him to cancel the date and promising to get in touch when she felt better, and wrote to the friend giving her the information, telling both that she had the flu. She called to cancel the dental appointment. Would you like to make another appointment? the receptionist asked. No, I'll call as soon as I'm up and about.

It was surprising how much energy these simple tasks demanded—before this week she'd been able to send a dozen emails in minutes without feeling the least bit weary. When she was done, she fell immediately asleep.

She remained in bed for two more days; the most active task she accomplished was making a grocery list and calling the supermarket for a delivery. Then she remembered she had tickets for a Saturday matinee with a friend; they were to have lunch first. She emailed to cancel that, blaming the flu.

She didn't neglect herself; she was not a sloppy or careless person, quite the contrary, known at work for her efficiency. She showered, brushed her teeth, and changed her nightgowns every day, and on the third day of rest she washed her hair. The apartment didn't need much attention; nevertheless, she called a cleaning service and arranged for someone to come in the next week. She wasn't going to let things go, just enjoy her rest for a few more days.

The man she'd been dating called to ask how she was and when they could get together. His low and slightly husky voice, one of the qualities that had first attracted her, left her unmoved. I think this might take a week or so, she said. I'll get in touch when I'm better. Have you seen a doctor? he said with concern. It was all she could do not to hang up abruptly—she hadn't had a real conversation in a while and found it strenuous. No, I'll be fine, she said. I'd better go now. I need to rest.

This pattern went on through the weekend and for several more days, and she began to wonder why she had been so assiduous for years about getting up and going about her affairs. In fact, very little was truly essential. Everyone dashed here and there, but was there any good reason for so much activity? Her own participation in the great world did not seem necessary, and it was so much more pleasant lying in bed dozing and reading. Of course, some people were truly essential, heads of state, for example. Or doctors who were saving lives. Sanitation men, plumbers. Maybe airline pilots, although where were all the passengers going? Did they really need to go?

Her assistant could easily do her job, for weeks if necessary, maybe longer. Nor did she feel lonely or crave company. When she was younger she had been a great reader, and now she took immense pleasure in reading, even rereading books she had loved. They were company enough. Friends had begun calling with concern, and while it was mildly pleasant to speak to them (though not as pleasant as resting), the calls were brief since she had no news to report. A couple of women she was close to had offered—she thought of it as threatened—to come over, but she discouraged them. They were suspicious. No doubt they would urge her to get out of bed and back to active life. They might even suggest therapy, assuming that she was depressed. There was no way to explain her present mode of life except to say that she enjoyed it.

She did not feel depressed; rather she felt an immense burden—something like a sack of gravel—being lifted from her, pebble by pebble, day by day. And as it lifted she also shed the tacit universal assumption of the need for action, for playing one's part in the busy world.

Of course there was the matter of money. She could not stay in bed indefinitely; she had a very small independent income but nowhere near enough to sustain her. She would have to see about taking a paid leave. Perhaps there was some work she could do from bed; she sometimes received emails advertising jobs of that sort. She'd always deleted them immediately, distrusting them, but they might be worth exploring. Meanwhile she could manage for several more weeks, perhaps even months, without worrying about money.

The man stopped calling. It didn't matter. If she ever got up, there would be other men. She tried to remember plans she had had in mind, things to do in the city, trips she hoped to take, but they had grown distant and lost their appeal. They would take effort, and her greatest wish—along with the wish not to be intruded upon—was not to expend any unnecessary effort. Her entire past life now struck her as an enormous expenditure of effort, and to what end she no longer understood. She did lack exercise and fresh air, it was true. Spring was coming; on warm days she opened the front window wide and stood breathing the balmy air wafting over from the trees. If she felt a great need she might go out for a walk one of these days. But not just yet.

Although she desired nothing more than to continue as she was, she knew that the day of reckoning would come. Before long she would be hearing from the higher-ups at work, who would demand that she clarify her intentions or lose her job. Friends would come by despite her discouraging them; they would bring flowers, food, and misguided counsel. She had stopped checking the calendar; no doubt there were appointments she hadn't shown up for. Even the dentist would start importuning her. Come back to the world, they would all say. It's where we belong.

And she would have to obey, in the end. She would begin keeping and adhering to the calendar once more. But with regret. With no conviction of necessity, except for a livelihood. Every night when she climbed into bed, the soft cocooned feeling would reawaken the memory of her prolonged rest, and the truths—not to mention pleasures—it had brought her.

Grief

At first there remained only ravaged images, those from her final weeks—the indignities of the body—images that she, so private and fastidious, would not have wanted included in the galleries of memory. He tried to banish them, like pulling down a window shade sharply over a scene of devastation. But the shade kept snapping up again, and in truth he took some perverse pleasure in looking through that window, however bleak the scene, because it was the only view he had. Then after a while, without his making any conscious effort—he was too stunned for effort—other images returned to him. Parts, not yet the whole person. Views of her, distorted, foreshortened, as she had looked sitting on his hips, on his chest, near his mouth. The odd planes and curves of such images, with folds where part met part, were like abstractions, or fractals. From those there gradually sprouted segments less erotically charged, her hair falling over a shoulder, the high arch of her foot, the slope and dip of her back. He tried to put them together to form a whole but could not. There were always parts missing, like the missing pieces in an old jigsaw puzzle, whose blank, irremediable spaces leave such disappointment and frustration.

Reluctantly, almost shamefaced, like a man who had hoped to accomplish a daunting task on his own but finds he cannot, he sought help. He unearthed old photographs.

They did help, restoring her face, smiling and flirting for the camera, or taken by surprise, with her look of expectant wariness. In one, he'd caught her reading in a hammock, brow furrowed, lips parted like a child's, hands gripping the book. Her fingers covered the title. He spent evenings going through the boxes of photographs, arranged haphazardly. She'd often said, half jokingly, that she would save the task of organizing them for her old age, when she wouldn't be able to do much else. But she never did get old enough to have time on her hands; and had she reached old age, he imagined she would still have had been busy, or pretended to be.

Certain phases of their lives and the children's lives were well documented—photos from outings, trips, birthday parties—while other patches were unrecorded: he didn't know why some and not others. For those empty patches he had to conjure up how she would have looked, what small changes in her face and body might have occurred since the last set of photos. Her hair might be shorter or longer, maybe a faint droop to her skin, a softening of the body though never a thickening.

They had friends who'd traced their son's appearance by taking a photo every month, from infancy until he left for college, all arranged consecutively in an album. The persistence of features was a revelation: month by month, despite the natural growth and change—the sharper definition of the face, the new contours of awareness inflected by the unseen events giving them shape—in essence the boy remained the same. Each month he resembled the boy of the month before, each year the boy of the year before, as if the young man had existed in a state of potential, waiting to unfold.

He wished he had a catalogue like that of her, month by month, even week by week. Then, with all the data he possessed, he could correlate her appearance with the milestones in their life and see how and if they had altered her: the various moves, changes of job, births of the children, failures and successes, marital crises and recuperations, all the vicissitudes that might or might not have left a physical trace, whose presence he, of all people, would be able to pinpoint.

Yet even without such a record, after some months, with the aid of the photos, he was satisfied that he had her back in his visual memory. From the early, wavering, fragmented images, he had her whole and solid and steady and could catalogue her transmutations. For close to a year, he had her in this way—everything except her tactile presence— and it was, as he had hoped, a consolation. Then a peculiar thing began to happen. As soon as he was confident that she could not be taken away, she started vanishing. Not the fading or blurring that comes with the passage of time. No, entire passages of her life simply fell away, leaving him with just a handful of discrete, arbitrary images, like signposts, sometimes freestanding, sometimes part of a scene. A moment on a Ferris wheel in Santa Monica—her look of surprise and apprehension as she gazed down from the top at the minuscule people below and the ocean beyond. The way she looked if he disturbed her at work, turning from the desk and raising her eyes with a willed patience shielding her impatience. Her face as she stood holding the phone, hearing of her father's sudden death, a look of insult, of grievance; in her other hand she was holding an eggplant.

There was less and less of her. Whatever revived when he looked at the photos vanished once he closed the album. What little remained, he imagined he carried around in a small safe whose combination he was in danger of forget-

ting. Maybe his faltering grasp of her was the inevitable re-
sult of love interrupted by death; or maybe it was simply
his memory floundering in the most ordinary way. Maybe
next time he opened the safe he'd find nothing but a small
mound of dust.

So it was that one morning, as he saw his grandson appear in the doorway—a silhouette backlit by bright sun—
and enter the room, taking on color and detail—ruddy face,
the crisp, colorful clothes of childhood—he thought of
how this boy, too, so very young, would eventually dissolve
into a clump of images, then dust. The boy came to him for
a greeting and he wanted to turn away, feeling, What's the
use? But he didn't, only hesitated an instant before hugging
the child. Because he loved him, certainly, but even more,
because he needed to maintain the collective pretense of
durability and significance. It would not do to act on what
he had discovered. Not that he hadn't known it before—everyone knows, fleetingly—but now he knew it differently:
viscerally, perpetually. To act on it could bring his life to
a standstill, and he was not ready for that. He must go on
pretending with all his might. One day he would forget he
was pretending; the pretense would become reality, and he
would return to what he had been before. He would rejoin
the world of the ignorant: that would be the end of active
grief.

Career Choice

The idea came to me after reading a novel written by an old man. The plot was simple: An old man, not in very good health, falls in love with a much younger woman. In fact, she falls in love with him first. Countless books and stories have been written on this theme. It must be the secret, or not so secret, dream of every old man. Its appeal is broad and deathless, though the dreamers may die—in the arms of the beloved, if possible. It helps if she is beautiful, but that is not essential. Youth is the crucial element. Even the most sophisticated of men, the wisest, the least likely to succumb to clichés, are not immune. It must be hard-wired in the brain, or somewhere.

So at a moment in my life when I had nothing and no one, when I had been in hiding for a while, so to speak, and badly needed a plan for the future, I decided on my goal. I was not extremely young, thirty-four, but young enough. I looked young, maybe because lately I'd lived apart from the fray. I'd spent the last several years taking care of my sister, my dear, sick sister, as she declined. After she died it took some time to clear out her things, do the paperwork, and so on. Now my future was a blank. And I lacked the strength of will for the world of computer dating that had overtaken my generation.

My experience nursing her was one qualification. Also, a few people in the past have called me beautiful, or parts of me, anyway, but in situations where some such comment is called for. I am not beautiful, but in my opinion striking, and I know how to make the most of my assets: I'm tall, olive-skinned, with enviable cheekbones, so that I've sometimes been mistaken for a Native American.

From what I'd read, I knew how I'd be expected to behave: affectionate, appreciative, helpful, encouraging. I couldn't know in advance what the sexual demands of the role would be—they were rarely detailed in the novels— but I trusted they wouldn't be beyond my abilities. In any event they couldn't be all that frequent.

What I wanted of the man I'd seek out was that he be clean, not violent, and sane, little enough to ask. Naturally with the passage of time those qualities might desert him, but they should be there to start with. Rich, it goes without saying, was the principal requirement, preferably without any close heirs. I have no special skills or talents and I used up most of my minuscule inheritance caring for my sister. The idea of looking for a job in my benumbed state of mind—and doing what?—was too daunting. I needed to be provided for when the time came, by which I mean his time, not mine, and at best not far off. Of course it would help if I liked him. But not too much. I'd had my fill of loss.

I thought of volunteering at a senior center—I could serve meals or lead a discussion group or exercise class. Even while caring for Jean I managed to get to the gym and to yoga classes. We had a wonderful hospice nurse, Georgette, an energetic older woman with a mop of grayish-blonde curls whose vitality lingered with us even after she left. Often she would stay an extra hour or two so I could get out. I could modify yoga to accommodate the aging. But on second thought I didn't pursue that. The kind of old man I sought wouldn't turn up there; he'd still be active in the world. Instead I enrolled in several classes at the local Y that might attract the right sort of person: one class on the history of the Broadway musical, one on FDR's New Deal, and finally—this was more of a lark, a treat for my efforts—in beginning Italian. I loved opera. Jean and I used to watch the televised performances from La Scala or the Met, sitting side by side on her bed.

The first two classes were not promising. The students were mostly women, and the few older men enrolled tended to fall asleep with their mouths open, especially during the Broadway tunes. They would wake up if called on or nudged by their neighbors, but soon drift off again. I stayed, though. I enjoyed the classes and you never knew who might turn up. Unexpectedly it was the Italian class I liked most.

I liked the teacher too. He was an Italian, a man who appeared to be in his late sixties, whose English was quite good, though he spoke with an accent. He was animated and peppered his lessons with jokes and anecdotes that kept us engaged, as well as with digressions on Italian history and art, geography and such. He liked to introduce idioms; for instance, when I answered a difficult question he called me a *ragazza in gamba*, but didn't know quite how to translate it. I looked it up later: smart girl, sharp, on the ball—but none of these captured the feel of the words.

He seemed well educated, maybe even had been a professor back in Italy. He was of medium height, quite trim, and had a kindly, almost handsome face, clean-shaven—I don't care for beards or mustaches—with abundant graying hair on the longish side. His face was weathered, as if he had spent time outdoors (a sea captain? forest ranger?) but the lines made him distinctive. His casual clothes seemed carefully chosen and expensive. His appearance reminded me of my father, who died of a stroke when I was in my twenties. I wondered if he was married. He didn't wear a ring, but then many European men don't. I noticed that on a trip to Europe I'd taken with my sister shortly before she fell ill. He was listed in the catalogue as Signor Barrochi but he said we should call him Signor Daniele.

I started going up to him at the end of class to ask questions about the evening's lesson, and he was warm and responsive. Why not give it a try? I had intended someone older and less robust, but I could be flexible. Anyone could get sick at any age—witness my poor sister, two years younger than I. Even if this teacher lasted a good while, I wouldn't mind his company. I was learning a lot. It was a small class, maybe a dozen, and aside from a few young male doctoral candidates preparing for language exams, all women, of whom I was by far the youngest. I was thinking about how to suggest coffee or a drink after class, or maybe recommend some Italian film in the neighborhood, when to my surprise he made the first move.

"Would you care for a glass of wine?" he said, after my question about when to use the subjunctive. To that he gave a dismissive but congenial wave of his hand, as if shunting aside a moth. Apparently the subjunctive was complicated and I shouldn't worry about it yet: we'd get to it later in the Beginners 2 class, if I cared to continue. As he hoped I would. Meanwhile, he said, there was a charming café just a block or two away. Of course I accepted.

It was a small place with Art Deco posters on the walls and banquette tables, so we settled in side by side as they do in Europe. I remembered that from our trip as well. The banquettes had looked uncomfortable to me, but my sister pointed out their advantages for intimacy. My teacher made a fuss about ordering just the right bottle of red wine, tasting it, pondering it, finally accepting it.

I didn't have to exert myself to make conversation because he was a big talker, like many men his age, or any age. All I needed to do was insert a few leading questions, and he was off and running.

He was Sicilian, from Palermo, and his wife had died about six years ago. He still had a son there, an engineer, married, and raising an orphaned niece of his wife's. He missed him terribly, being so far away, but he'd needed a major change after his wife's death. He had been quite depressed—at this I felt a twinge of doubt. A depressive was more than I was prepared to handle. One of my college boyfriends was depressed and I found it hard to be sympathetic with his moodiness and indolence. Why should I be made miserable just because he was?

As I suspected, my teacher had been a professor of history, and came to the States with the promise of a job teaching languages at an East Side private school in New York. His new life revived his spirits and he had been fine ever since. Good news. I admired his pluck, willing to start over in strange surroundings at a fairly advanced age. Now he gave occasional lectures, did translations, and found teaching gigs of the kind he did at the Y. He had left his job at the school a year ago. "A friend found me that job," he said. "I didn't need it to live, but I didn't want to come with no plan, you understand. I wasn't ready to . . . *piantar cavoli...*" I must have looked puzzled because he smiled and added, "It's an idiom. Retire. Plant cabbages, tend to my garden, like Candide. I needed some place to go every day, and that saved me. Then, once I was saved, I was free to do whatever I pleased."

From this I got the impression that he didn't need the money, that he had a good bit stashed away. But where? In

Italy? Was it accessible? But such questions were premature.

I liked his hands. They were large, with long fingers and impeccably groomed fingernails. They moved restlessly on the table as he spoke. They were creased, as happens to old people, but not unappealing.

Finally he stopped talking and looked me in the eye. "I am boring you, I'm afraid. Tell me something of you, now. What brings you to this class?"

I assured him I wasn't bored but fascinated. I told him the minimum about myself—in fact there wasn't much to tell. I'd been raised in New York City, where my parents were public-school teachers. After college I worked as a personal assistant for a successful writer of cookbooks. The job was lively. My office was next to the large kitchen and I often joined the cook and her helpers, whose work seemed like play, with much fooling around, cooking up the leftovers and eating them. After a while I thought I should get serious about the future, and took a job as assistant to the director of a nonprofit agency in the field of child welfare. When my sister got sick I left it to care for her. Both my parents were gone by then, within a few months of each other, leaving Jean and me on our own. I told him my sister had died recently from a neurological disease. She had started out as a dancer but the illness made it impossible for her to dance or do much of anything. It was a cruel disease. Now, like him, I said, I needed a change, but couldn't afford anything so extreme as moving to another country. All of this was true—I had no intention of lying during my quest, except perhaps about matters of the heart.

His condolences seemed sincere and were not excessive. My few words satisfied him and soon he was off again on the subject of his impressions of New York City, an inexhaustible subject. After a few moments I looked at my watch and said I should be going. He offered to take me home in a taxi but I said I lived close enough to walk and had a few errands along the way.

"So perhaps we might do this again," he said, "if you are not too occupied."

I was certainly not very occupied, but didn't say that. I simply thanked him, said I liked his taste in wine, and would be glad to do this again.

Things moved along fairly swiftly. Before long he was smitten—to use an archaic word he might have used had he known it. I could sense that. And I was enjoying his company.

* * *

"How is it you're not married?" he asked one night after class, in his favorite café. By this time we had had dinner several times and been to a couple of classic Italian films. *The Leopard*, with Burt Lancaster as the aging prince. *L'Avventura*. He had good taste. "A beautiful young woman like you. Or perhaps you have a..." He paused, seeking the right word. I wouldn't have been surprised if he said something like "suitor" or "beau." "Companion," he finally came up with. "Boyfriend" was not his kind of word.

"I guess the right opportunity never came along. I have nothing against marriage. But it has to be to a suitable person."

"And... what would a suitable person be like?"

I smiled, I hoped not coyly. "I couldn't say, until it happens." I drank some more wine for courage.

"And could a suitable person be a much older man?"

"It might. It depends." More wine. Cut to the chase. "Are you referring to yourself?"

"I am. I've fallen in love with you. You must know that,

don't you? *Sono innamorato di te.* I want to marry you, Samantha." He had trouble with the "th" but tried valiantly.

I had read ahead in our Italian textbook and come upon the various ways of saying "I love you" in Italian, which were more subtle than in English. *Ti amo* means "I love you" in the way we use it, between lovers. *Essere innamorato,* to be in love, means the same, but in a more erotic, heady way, as at the beginning of an affair, which is how Daniele was using it. And then, to complicate matters, there is *ti voglio bene,* which means "I love you" or "I care for you," but is used also with family and close friends, and does not necessarily imply romantic or sexual love, though it might. I wanted to answer properly. I couldn't honestly say I loved him or was in love with him, and even *ti voglio bene* felt too strong for our situation.

I had the absurd urge to thank him. I don't think anyone had truly been in love with me before, not enough to want to spend a lifetime with me. But I controlled the urge. "I'm flattered," I said. "I'm not sure I deserve your love. You're a much more..." I didn't know how to go on. "You're a much more cultivated person than I. I mean you've lived longer and done so much more." But what was I saying? Candor could go too far. I didn't want to turn him off.

"That has nothing to do with love," he said in Italian, and gave that dismissive wave again. "*Non c'entra.* You're a *persona per bene.*"

I didn't get that.

"A good person," he explained. "A ... what? An honorable person."

That was exactly what I was not, in this situation. I had no illusions about what I was doing.

"How can you be sure? We barely know each other."

There was a long pause. This time Daniele sipped wine.

"That is true. So maybe you will come home with me tonight and then we will know each other better."

A night spent together might reveal much, but not whether I was a good person, a *persona per bene*. I didn't bother pointing this out; surely he knew it.

We had done nothing more than exchange a light kiss when we parted after our evenings together. He was ever the gentleman, a throwback to an earlier time. His lips were full and soft and I liked the feel and smell of him. But a night together would reveal so much more. I hesitated. I had to remind myself this was precisely what I had hoped for. My future could be assured and undemanding. I might even have loved him, were he several decades younger. *Ti voglio bene*, I thought. I care for you. Why was I hesitating? I should be glad of my success.

I was afraid. I hadn't taken my clothes off for anyone for several years. For anyone new, that is. I had an old friend from my days at the nonprofit agency, a man who would sometimes come by when my sister was alive. Neither of us was serious about it—for old times' sake, we always said. I had resolved to end this friendship if I married. Although it crossed my mind, I confess, that that might depend on what Daniele was like as a lover. I had every desire and intention to be a faithful wife, and I hoped for the best.

He should be the jittery one, I told myself. I was young and in excellent shape. But what would he expect? What would an Italian of his age and background want to do in bed, exactly? Probably just the usual. It couldn't be something I'd never dreamed of. I could always say no. I was sure he wouldn't insist.

I recognized that this train of thought was absurd. "I like that idea," I said, though it felt too much like an audition. His or mine? "And I've been curious about your house. I don't even know where you live."

He lived in a handsome old brick building—so far spared by the developers—on New York's Upper East Side, not far from my own apartment but in a better section. We went there in a taxi. In the taxi he took my hand and brought it to his lips. We kissed, more seriously than before. But that was all. He was too dignified to grope in the back seat of a taxi like a teenager or a character in a Hollywood movie.

From the little I could see as we entered, the apartment was large and expensively furnished, colorful, softly lit. I wondered if he had chosen the things himself or hired a decorator. I might ask later, depending on how things went. He spent no time showing me around, but led me right to the large bedroom, curtained and carpeted, where he undressed me slowly, starting with the light jacket I wore, then the earrings, very deftly, the belt and the boots, taking care with each item, and on to the rest. He undressed quickly. I stretched out on the bed in odalisque fashion and stole glances at his body. It was a good body, worn but strong. Muscular, mildly hairy. Maybe he frequented the gym too. He had a young man's erection, formidable, yet he took his time. Though what would I know about old men's erections? I liked the way he approached me. I liked him. It wasn't love, but it was good. He was a man who liked women—not always the case. The ones who like women are aroused by their responses; the others barely notice, so intent on their own pleasure. As he embraced me I wondered about his Sicilian wife. Had she been a dark-haired beauty like Claudia Cardinale in *The Leopard*, or was she like poor Burt Lancaster's dried-up, pinch-lipped wife? Pondering this was distracting, so I stopped.

Daniele asked for nothing, but wanted to please me. I

was too distracted and anxious to be thoroughly pleased, I couldn't let go enough. I pretended ecstasy, and he was pleased with himself; that was what I'd hoped to accomplish. I couldn't tell whether he'd worried about making a good showing. He seemed quite at his ease. I did know that this was something I need not dread if I accepted his proposal. On the contrary.

The bed was large and comfortable and I slept soundly. For an instant I was startled to find his head next to mine in the morning. "Do you still want to marry me?" I asked, as if it had been my audition, not his.

"*Ma certo*. Of course I do. Even more."

"*Ti voglio bene*," I said. And we made love again and this time I wasn't too distracted to enjoy it. There would be no need to contact my old friend.

*   *   *

We resolved to have a civil ceremony by ourselves. Daniele's son and his wife were not flying over to attend. "Gabriele is very busy," he said after a phone call, trying to hide his disappointment. Instead we would celebrate afterwards with a few friends of his I had already met and liked.

"So tell me," he said as we left the county clerk's office and headed towards the Italian restaurant he had chosen, "why would a beautiful young woman like you want to marry an old man like me? I'm not even rich," he added ironically.

We had never discussed money, or only just enough for me to grasp that there would be no need for me to work. I understood that he was testing me and that I mustn't even flutter an eyelid. I had spent enough time in the co-op apartment, with its seven rooms and elegant furnishings— yes, chosen with the help of a decorator— to know this was his idea of a joke.

"That doesn't matter," I joked back. "I'm rich. I'll take care of you."

He laughed. He had been in my modest apartment, the small place Jean and I had gotten after our parents' deaths, helping me pack and sort through the few things I wanted. He had surely noted my circumstances.

"Speaking of old," I whispered during our celebratory lunch, emboldened by the rich food and wine, and the fact that the deed was done, "you've never actually told me how old you are. Are you afraid?"

"I am afraid of nothing, *cara*. Seventy-one. Does that surprise you?" He tapped on his glass for a toast.

"A little. You do look younger." More than twice my age. I felt a slight chill. What had I done? But this was what I'd planned. Older should be better. "Oh, what does age matter anyway?" I murmured.

The guests joined in the toast. "*La mia metà*," Daniele said. My better half. I had already met his close friend and attorney, Carlo, and his wife, a financial adviser. The others were a pair of gay men who designed scenery for the theater, and a New York–based journalist for an Italian newspaper and her husband. I was worried about how these educated, worldly people would regard me, but they were kind and accepting. They kept the conversation in English for my benefit, and were appreciative when I attempted a few simple Italian phrases. "*Che bellezza! Brava* for the bride!" they shouted. "Good accent." A shaft of sunlight shone through the window near our table, brightening the faces around me. I was happy.

Certain things about our future had already been settled. Daniele did not want more children, and I had no desire to be a young widow with a small child. Naturally

I didn't put it in those words. What I wanted to do, after getting my bearings and recovering from the years of nursing and losing my sister, my dearest friend in the world, was travel, either with Daniele or without him. I hadn't been anywhere except for that one trip with Jean. I lingered over brochures that came in the mail offering trips to Mexico, to Scotland, to Morocco. Perhaps we would go to Italy and I could speak Italian. To my surprise there was not much opportunity to improve my Italian with Daniele because he preferred English. He was eager to perfect his English and always stopped to question me if I uttered an unfamiliar word or phrase. When he asked if I could help him install his new printer, I said, "Of course. Piece of cake," and I had to explain what that meant. He took a fancy to the phrase and used it when he could.

This matter of language almost caused a disagreement between us in the early weeks. I had finished the Beginners 1 class at the Y and wanted to enroll in his section of Beginners 2. But he said that would be awkward. "I won't be able to concentrate properly with my wife in the class."

"But why on earth not? People won't know we're married."

"People always know. And then . . . aren't there rules about students and teachers? Americans are so strict about such things.'"

I laughed. "Those rules are for colleges and universities, or corporate executives and assistants, not for adult classes like yours. Have no fear, no one will think you took advantage of me." If anything it was I who had taken advantage of him. Even once I explained, he was adamant. He had no objection to my taking the class with another teacher or continuing my studies elsewhere, so I gave in. I didn't want to cause a rift, when we were getting along so well. "Okay.

I suppose having me in the class would be like a busman's holiday for you."

"A busman's holiday?" he repeated. "What does that mean?"

"It's an idiom. It means that what you do on your vacation is the same as the work you're vacationing from. Like, suppose your job is leading groups on hiking trips, and then on your vacation you go hiking."

"But what if hiking is what you love to do?" He didn't appreciate the analogy; I might have explained it better. Later on I looked it up. The expression originated in nineteenth-century England when buses were drawn by horses. If the drivers took a vacation they usually had to travel by horse-drawn bus.

*   *   *

I sometimes wondered what Jean, an ardent feminist, would think of the path I had taken. She might have been appalled. Or the opposite—admired my resourcefulness. In any event she couldn't accuse Daniele of predatory behavior; his manners were impeccable, even after we married. Beyond manners, I was discovering that he had what our mother had quaintly called "character." Remember, girls, she said when we started seeing boys, it's not the surface that matters. Character is more important. Jean and I would roll our eyes. Now, as I got to know the neighbors in my new home, I found everyone had a good word for Daniele, his generosity and kindness.

I settled into an easy life. There was household help, naturally, a middle-aged woman named Gemma, from Turin, who was reliable and good-natured. She was devoted to Daniele. He was *buonissimo*, she said. When she'd told him about her son, who was a bit "slow," she confided, he arranged for a scholarship at a special school. I had a suspicion that this "scholarship" came directly from Daniele.

So, no need for me to lug around a vacuum, though I wouldn't have minded, but I did keep things in order. As housemates we were well suited. I was orderly by nature and so was Daniele. Wet towels or newspapers scattered on the floor might have made me regret my hasty decision. He liked me to dress well and gave me two credit cards, which I didn't overuse. My usual jeans and shirts would not do for the restaurants he liked or for the opera. One of the surprise benefits of our marriage was a subscription to the Met. I looked forward to the time when I would understand the Italian and not need to consult the English translations flashed onto the seat in front of me.

To my surprise, besides possessing character, he liked fancy underwear. "I have pictured you in black lace," he whispered one night as I undressed. This was after a month or so, as if he had been too shy to express the wish before. There was no reason not to indulge him, and though I was amused by some of the outlandish creations in the lingerie departments, I bought a good supply. The satin felt lovely against my skin but the gauzy lace could be itchy. At first I felt a bit silly wearing them, but I got accustomed to it. It was worth it. Just looking at it, or me in it, aroused him. He liked me to stand in front of the full-length mirror—the bedroom was full of mirrors, something else he liked—while he fondled and tongued until he finally ripped the things off me. "Look," I once said afterwards, holding up a shredded pair of black lace panties, "look what you've done."

"Buy more," he said.

Sometimes we ended up on the floor. His excitement excited me and I came quickly, always before he did, and

without even thinking, I whispered, "*Ti amo, ti amo.*"
Speaking the Italian words aroused me, but he preferred to
hear it in English, the language of his new life. I complied; I
did whatever he wanted. He was living an old man's dream,
and I was the dream. I suspected that I was living a dream
too, a dream of being passive and effortlessly adored.

Those were memorable nights, more than I had bar-
gained for, and they unsettled me. I had anticipated a great
deal about what living with him might be like, and in most
aspects I was right. The one thing I had not anticipated was
passion. Mine, I mean. I had imagined that making love
with Daniele would be rather like a gesture of goodwill on
my part. Instead, what I felt was unnerving.

Like everyone else I had dipped into Freud in college;
it didn't escape me that my orgasms might erupt from some
buried and dubious source. But I thought not. My relations
with my father had been lukewarm, an affectionate lack of
interest on both sides. Jean had been his favorite. No, Daniele's body was real, the man I was responding to. I never
had to resort to fantasies, as I occasionally had with men
before: reality now was so much like a fantasy, only tangible, tactile, on the skin.

It was growing difficult to keep my original plan in mind,
conceived with a cold heart: to be a good and faithful wife,
and to wait. Those nights of pleasure left me restless, like an
adolescent beset by unaccustomed feelings. Daniele was busy
with teaching and translating. I needed occupation as well. I
told him I wanted to find work. I thought he might not like
the idea, but my worry turned out to be needless.

"I'm not surprised, Sami. So what do you know how
to do? Or, what else can you do, I should say," he added
with an amused smile, but I was not in the mood for erotic
banter.

I didn't like to admit how lacking I was in practical skills. It struck me that he had married me knowing very little about me. It had been a greater leap of faith for him than for me. For my part, I saw my limitations all too clearly. In this era of women's independence, how could I find myself this way, useless, without ambition? I hadn't been like this when I was younger. It must have been the years of inertia and grief, my parents and sister slipping away one by one.

"I had an administrative job once, for a few years. I managed the office, but it was quite small. Organizing, public relations, networking . . ." In retrospect it seemed I hadn't done much. "I worked for a woman who wrote cookbooks, remember, I once told you. I know how to take care of sick people, but I don't want to do that again. It was only because it was my sister and there was no one else."

"I'll look around, maybe I know someone."

"I want to find it myself," I said petulantly, like a child.

"Of course, *cara*. You can do . . . the computer?"

Beyond the simplest procedures, this was baffling to Daniele, especially in English. "Yes, I can do that. But I don't like it."

"What do you like?"

"I like learning Italian."

He laughed. "That's not a job, Sami." He had taken to calling me that—trying to pronounce Samantha defeated him.

It had been a job, for me.

In the end I found something on my own, working in a Chelsea art gallery that specialized in photography. They needed someone who would look good at the front desk, greet visitors, answer the phone, update the website, and follow up with interested patrons. I told them to call me Sami—I had come to like it. It was an easy job, three days a week, mildly interesting work with no future. But I no longer had to worry about the future. Now that I had accomplished my goal I just needed something to occupy me every day. I was far too young to plant cabbages. The gallery handled mostly new and innovative photographers. I enjoyed looking at their work and chatting with them, but discouraged any who tried to get friendly. I wasn't even tempted.

Daniele was glad that I had found something suitable and undemanding. Meanwhile I had completed the second Beginners course and was now enrolled in Intermediate. I was eager to speak Italian with Daniele, simple conversations that I could manage, and though he would indulge me for a while, he was not enthusiastic.

"What is it?" I asked. "Is my accent too painful to listen to, or my grammar?"

"No, no, you do fine." He waved his hand in the air. "But it's a busman's holiday, remember you taught me that phrase?"

In my spare time I learned to cook Italian food. I thought back to what I had learned in my first job, which was more than I had realized. We invited his friends over for dinner and he was proud of me, especially as I had mastered a superb osso buco. I was contented, or as close as someone like me could come to contentment. I could have continued in this way indefinitely.

*   *   *

We had been married for almost a year and planned to celebrate our anniversary by giving a party. Catered, of course. Daniele wouldn't dream of my taking on so much work, though I was willing. It was at the party that he started feeling ill, and I thought that he must have drunk too much or eaten something unfamiliar. The party went well, jovial and lively, lots of food and music, even dancing—he turned out to be a good dancer. But his face had a grayish hue that alarmed me. He stuck it out to the end and said goodbye to the guests with his usual grace. As soon as they were gone he fell into bed with barely a word. I pulled off his shoes. He waved away my offer to help and said not to worry, he'd be fine in the morning. "Just a little below the weather."

But he wasn't simply under the weather. Before long there were more bad days than good; there were headaches and dizziness. He lost weight. After he fell several times he consented to see a doctor, and then began the inevitable series of tests. There was nothing to be done, we were told. It was too late. "Try to keep him comfortable," the doctor advised as he handed over the prescriptions. How often had I heard those words when it was Jean?

Daniele wanted to hire a live-in nurse. "This is too terrible for you, *cara. Un boccone amaro.*" A bitter pill. "I don't want you to go through it. You've barely . . . what do you say . . . *ristabilita* . . . got over from your sister's death."

"Gotten over," I corrected. I would never get over it, nor this, but it was pointless to say so.

I insisted I could care for him. I didn't want a stranger in the house, aside from Gemma. She was easy to have around and could help. I had vowed for better or for worse and I would do what must be done, even though worse had come so soon. I had fantasies that it might pass, that the doctors were wrong, or they would discover a miraculous way to restore him. It was intolerable to see him weakened, diminished, slipping out of my grasp. I grew angry at what I had planned so cleverly. I even felt an obscure guilt, as though my scheming had brought him to this point. Would he be sick if he had never met me? At the beginning I had

had power and control and used them. Now, though my desires had reversed—I wished us more time together—I had no control over this ending. There was rarely a need for the fancy satin and lace anymore, but I still wore it at night; I was used to it, and he liked to run his hands over me, even in his sleep.

Though it was becoming arduous, he got up and dressed most days and fussed over papers on his desk in the study. One morning he called me over and motioned me to sit down.

He began abruptly. "You'll have the apartment, naturally, and everything in it."

"Please, Daniele. Must we talk this way? You seem a bit better. You even look better today."

His hand sliced across the air. "*I miei giorni sono contati.* Listen to me now."

His days are counted? Oh. His days are numbered, he was saying.

"And enough money. You'll consult Carlo about that." I had gotten to know his attorney, Carlo, fairly well; he had been over for dinner several times and appreciated my cooking. "The house in Palermo and the land will be for Gabriele, of course."

House? Land? I'd never heard of them before. "Of course," I echoed.

"Carlo will take care of everything for you."

I started to cry and he reached out to offer me a handkerchief. "*Peccato.* A pity," he said gently, "that you let yourself come to love me."

*   *   *

A week or so later he was spending most of his time in bed. He refused to go to a hospital. He told me he had emailed his son, and Gabriele and his wife would be arriving in a few days.

I got a spare bedroom ready and prepared an Italian dinner to welcome them. Daniele hadn't told me much about Gabriele so I didn't know what to expect. Trembling with anxiety, I opened the door to a tall, burly man in his early forties, already balding. Daniele had plenty of hair; they say baldness is passed down through the mother. He was pulling two large suitcases, and his wife, a plump woman with dyed auburn hair, dragged another. Her pants were too tight and her heels too high and her lipstick too red, and she regarded me as though I were a butler. I disliked her on sight. To my surprise, they were followed by a young woman I hadn't noticed at first. She resembled the beautiful Claudia Cardinale as I recalled her from *The Leopard,* and looked about nineteen or twenty. Of course, she must be the wife's niece. Daniele hadn't told me she was coming too.

Benvenuti, I greeted them, and did my best to smile. They replied in English. In my fantasies they threw their arms around me with the warmth Italians are reputed to possess. This of course did not happen; I'd never truly expected it. Gabriele shook my hand. "Samantha," he said formally, struggling over the "th" as Daniele had done. His voice was much like Daniele's, deep and soft, and it sounded odd coming from such a large man.

"Call me Sami."

His wife, Elvira, gazed around at the furnishings appraisingly. The girl was introduced as Mariana; she looked around as well, wide-eyed, as if awed by the surroundings.

They asked to see Daniele right away, so I ushered them into the bedroom where he lay resting, and then backed away. They surrounded the bed and bent to embrace him. I heard Elvira say he was "*magro come un chiodo,*" thin as a nail—or as we would say, a rail. A moment later came loud insistent chatter, but I could barely understand it. They were speaking too fast for me, or maybe using a Sicilian dialect.

I left and prepared a room for Mariana, and once they were settled in I returned to Daniele. I sat beside him on the bed and took his hand. "You haven't seen him in so long," I said. "Has he changed a lot?"

"Heavier. Older. Losing his hair."

"Yes." For the first time in his company, I didn't know what to say. He had suddenly acquired a history and a context, a textured, rooted past that had previously had the feeling of a faraway myth, like the ancient myths I learned about in school. He was changed, not only because of the illness, but changed as if enclosed in a kind of caul that placed him beyond my touch. "You didn't tell me the niece was coming."

"She goes to nursing school. I thought she could help you."

"Help me? I don't need help. Haven't I been managing all right? And aren't there nurses right here in New York?" I stopped. This was no time for bickering, and bickering had never been our style.

"I want to make this easier for you, *cara*. Not a piece of cake, I know. Now you can go out. Even go back to your job."

I had left the job after we found out how sick he was, and barely thought of it since. But I said nothing. Their voices drifted in from the living room. Everything would be different now.

"I'll go and offer them some coffee," and I kissed him quickly and left the room.

*   *   *

Over the following days they made no effort to hide that they regarded me as an interloper. They accepted my services, the meals and so on, but not my attempts to be friendly. Only the girl, Mariana, was approachable. I offered to take her for walks through the city, but she seemed reluctant to venture out of the apartment. The first day or so she stayed in her room and watched television.

I had keys made for Gabriele and Elvira, who came and went as they pleased. It was a relief to have them out of the house. Gabriele often spent time in the bedroom with Daniele, while I wondered what they talked about. Not me, I hoped. Did Gabriele object to me and did Daniele have to defend me? Explain that I'd turned out well, like some waif picked up on the street?

Elvira was more curious to see New York but declined when I suggested places we might go together. The only times she addressed me were to ask about shopping. I mentioned a shop that sold excellent Italian shoes, but she said she could find plenty of Italian shoes at home, and cheaper.

Even Gemma, our housekeeper, who came every other day, was appalled by their aloofness. She liked to help me with Italian and we had developed a comradely bond. We took to exchanging quick comments about Gabriele and Elvira, like kids whispering in corners about the teacher. *Ci mancava anche questa*, she said—this was the last thing we needed. She was on my side, I thought with relief. But how awful to think of our once peaceable household as divided into sides.

Carlo came by a few times. He would sit with Daniele for a while, then he and Gabriele would go into the study and close the door for a couple of hours. I always urged that he stay for dinner, because dinner, for me, had become a painful ritual. Gabriele and Elvira would speak to each other, while Mariana and I tried valiantly to converse, but she was shy and her English was minimal. Carlo, who was talkative and genial, would include me in the conversation, and I hoped that might change things. And indeed, Gabriele and Elvira were civil while he was there, but when he left the frostiness resumed. They would go to sit with Daniele while Mariana and I loaded the dishwasher.

I longed to shout at them: I've been good to him. His first wife has been gone for years. So why . . . ? How stupid I was. It took me longer than it should have to understand it was more than my newness and youth. It was about money. If I had had money of my own I would gladly have thrown Daniele's wealth in their faces. Living with him in intimacy, finding him the *persona per bene* that he was, I let myself forget that the money had been my object at the start. This was simply my life now, one I had chosen and owned. How dare these strangers wish to dispossess me?

As Daniele declined he needed more care, and Mariana gradually took over what she knew better than I. Now it was she who handled the morning and evening routines, and who sometimes sat with him in the afternoons. When I entered the room and heard them speaking in their rough-sounding dialect, I felt superfluous and slipped away. If he was alone, he would often ask me to call her. She was a gentle, sweet-natured girl, attentive to Daniele and helpful and respectful to me. I tried hard not to resent her for being younger than I, and more beautiful, and for speaking his native tongue.

Illness changes people in unexpected ways, as I knew from caring for Jean, but I didn't anticipate the change coming over Daniele. As his health deteriorated so did his English. Or, as his illness advanced, his English retreated. I tried speaking to him in Italian as best as I could, but he wasn't as patient or indulgent with my efforts as he used to be. It was as if the illness had stripped away the recent layers of English to reveal his childhood dialect, like layers of paint stripped away to uncover an old masterpiece. He was not reverting to childhood in other ways, as the dying sometimes do. His mind was the same as ever; he followed the news on television, he talked to Gabriele and of course to Mariana. I was the person he seemed to need least. Maybe, like his English, I was part of a layer too recent to have much significance now. Those early days when he was so charmed seemed to have faded, for him, to a mere streak of color.

I had learned to tolerate Gabriele and Elvira's coldness, but I could not bear Daniele's withdrawal. This was the man who had stood behind me at the bedroom mirror and taken my clothes off as if he were unwrapping a gift.

I arranged for hospice care. I gasped when the hospice nurse appeared at the door. It was the same nurse who had come for Jean, Georgette with her unruly mop of curls. She was shocked as well.

"Samantha! I never dreamed I'd see you again . . . like this. Is it your father now?"

"My husband," I said. She must cover this neighborhood, I realized.

"Oh, I didn't know you got married. I'm so sorry about this. I didn't expect . . . from the data I was given I thought it was an older person."

When I led her to our bedroom and she saw Daniele, surprise washed over her face like a film but she said nothing. She came every few days with her painkillers, and in spite of the memories she revived, I looked forward to her visits. She was another person in the house on my side.

One day she paused in the bedroom doorway, turned back, and motioned to me to enter. Daniele was lying propped up on pillows, asleep. On my side of the bed, beside him, lay Mariana. They were holding hands. When she heard us enter she opened her eyes and sprang up.

"Forgive me, Signora Sami," she said. "*Mi dispiace tanto.* Signor Daniele ... he asked me. He's so good, I didn't like to refuse him. Please, it was nothing. He just wanted to hold my hand." She raised her hand as if to prove her innocence. She was practically in tears. I understood: I had never liked to refuse him either. And I felt sorry for her. How could she know she was an archetype, that she embodied an old man's dream? Even better than I.

"All right, all right, no harm done," Georgette said. "Leave us now and I'll take his vitals."

I left too. I got my purse and went out.

After that Mariana avoided me, blushing whenever she saw me. I would lower my eyes, ashamed of my jealousy. I lay beside Daniele in bed every night, half-awake in case he needed anything. Looking back, maybe I should have asked Mariana to lie next to him instead and hold his hand. That would have been a generous act, the act of a *persona per bene,* but more than I was capable of. He lasted a few more days, which I spent walking the streets and going to movies. Georgette took care of the details. Gabriele and Elvira said they wanted his body shipped back to Palermo. I didn't object. I looked into the arrangements, but they were so complicated that I couldn't face them. I asked Carlo to handle it.

When it was all over, Gabriele and Elvira packed their bags. They shook hands as they left, but I hugged Mariana and kissed her on both cheeks as the Italians do. The house was silent and empty. I was left with my sexy underwear and expensive furnishings and the mirrors. I avoided looking in the mirrors, as if they retained the images they had witnessed.

Near November

The terrible mocking blue sky is finally gone and we are all glad, even the obedient ones who have taken up their daily rounds, pretending life will be as before. The sky has paled, the warmth drained from the air, and still we come each morning with our boxes of chalk, our knee-pads, our goggles. We need to be down here; it's where we belong, we're pulled to the barricaded streets. The foul air makes us cough but the searing in our throats spurs us on. The first morning after, only a few of us came, all with the same idea, to write in big letters on the streets. With every passing morning, those blazing azure mornings, others joined us. At first the police looked askance, then decided we were harmless. People stop to ask why we are down on our hands and knees, why two months later we keep writing on the streets. Sometimes they join us.

We write the same thing each day: I was in my car, on the bridge, I saw ... On the bus, a woman on a cell phone started screaming ... I was feeding the baby, I had the radio on... The phone rang, it was my sister-in-law, my girlfriend, my downstairs neighbor, my ex-husband ... I was in the coffee shop, at the office, at the dentist, in class, from my hospital bed I saw it all out the window . . . I was in Honolulu, in London, in Paris, in Sydney . . .

The city sent people to question us. They were gentle, at least at first. Everyone was gentle, at first. We were breaking no laws. It is not yet against the law to write on the streets. It would be hard to arrest us anyway—we are too many. Now at night, to deter us, they hose the streets down. (It seems never to rain anymore, as if the sky holds back its tears.) See, they say, your writing is washed away. No matter. We'll write it again: The butcher's wife was in there. The girl in my yoga class was in there. The super's daughter. My daughter. My father. My wife.

A man from the city pleaded with us: Go back to your lives, he said. Or at least write something new.

We would like to write something new, we are very tired of our stories, but we don't know what the next sentence should be.

We have tried to proceed to the next sentence. But to write, you must know something, and we know nothing beyond the intolerable questions that assail us. Grief, at an infernal temperature, has burnt knowledge out of us. We try to write the next sentence, and senseless, contrary words come out, as if from a cauldron. What is the just path? Revenge is tempting, but also loathsome and useless. Can we love our country if we cannot love the voices that claim to be our country? Could this have happened? Look, over there, it happened. Terrible things have always happened to people. Why not to us? But why should such things happen to anyone? Who did it? Who are "they"? Who is innocent? Who is guilty? How can we tell? Is it war again? Then win the war. But don't kill anyone. Be prudent. No, be bold. No, a show of strength will only make things worse. The voices that blame us stir our rage—this is no time for blaming. The voices that extol us stir our rage—this is no time for smugness. Will some voice, please, speak an intelligent word in public? We long to hear an intelligent word. No, we long for silence. Enough words have been spoken. The words are ashes poured in our ears. Deafened, we seek the right path. But with our eyes coated with ash, how can we see any path, or truth, or justice?

We cannot write such sentences, made of useless words that seethe in the head. Of that blue and fire morning, we can only write what we know for certain: I would have been in there except I slept late . . . I had a toothache . . . I got caught in traffic . . .

But our sisters . . . Our brothers . . .

This we imprint on the streets, as if the soft chalk might cut grooves in the pavement. We cling to our stories, we take root in our stories like the nymph took root in a tree and became its prisoner. Unlike her, we will regain our shapes—almost. We will do what is needed; we will write the next sentence. Only not yet, not here on the bleak brink of November.

A Taste of Dust

Diving up from the city, Violet had imagined the house was substantial, but hadn't envisioned this bay-windowed, white mansion in miniature set far back from the curving suburban street. Large elms shaded the lawn; the hedges were expertly trimmed; too late for many flowers in October, but lots of shrubs. Definitely a hired gardener, or else Cindy had an unusually green thumb. Little in that line could be expected of Seth, unless he'd changed drastically and become a devotee of the Home Depot in the mall a few miles back. An SUV loomed in the broad driveway; she pulled up behind it. There would be a dog too, she guessed, a big one. Any minute it might come bounding across the lawn. She steeled herself. She'd pat it and not shrink from the paws clawing at her slate-blue silk suit, bought especially for the occasion, to show off her undefeated body and long legs.

An instant after she rang, as if he'd been waiting behind the door, there was Seth, restraining the dog by its collar. Violet fussed over the animal to give herself more time. A white and amber collie, prototypical faithful Lassie, it sniffed her with cordial interest, a contented dog.

"Violet! It's been so long. You look marvelous!"

She forced herself to look up. "Thank you." She couldn't say the same, even to be polite. It would be too blatant a lie. What she had managed to stave off these sixteen years had conquered him. He had passed the threshold of the country of the old, gone soft, and begun to shrink and stoop. His face was pouchy. His jaw had lost its clean, firm line. His lips were thinner, tighter. At this age, one either crossed that border abruptly—overnight—or was granted, by luck or genes or time spent at the gym, a few more years of being presentable. Seth, never athletic, wasn't one of the lucky ones. His clothes were still good, expensive and pressed, though they couldn't hang with the same grace. They would have suited him better had they been wrinkled. The shirt was deep blue, always his best color, though Violet couldn't help imagining the flesh beneath, sagging, folding on itself, with a pale, lifeless tinge.

He bent down to kiss her cheek and hug her awkwardly. She sympathized: how do you hug an ex-wife? She'd anticipated this moment and wondered if the mere brush of bodies could revive years of intimacy. It could. He was the naked man who had bent over her night after night, until he stopped. The inimitable scent and feel of ancient sex embalmed hit like a rush of stale hot air on her skin. She drew back as soon as she decently could.

Behind Seth, Cindy, once the secret girlfriend and now the anointed wife, waited in the spacious foyer, uncertain what to do with her arms. They were opened—bare, taut, and pink—but not quite wide enough to hug, ready for whatever Violet was ready for. Tucked snugly in her beige slacks and shirt, Cindy served her time at the gym, no doubt about that. Violet had seen her only in snapshots that the children, bitter and out of sorts after their weekend visits long ago, used to thrust in front of her, inviting her disdain, which she refused to give. They showed a curly-haired, rosy, rounded Cindy. Cute. Violet had never been cute or cuddly. Sleek and smooth and dark. Elegant when young, and now becoming stately as well.

Today's Cindy had outgrown cuteness. Violet's interest was purely clinical by now, yet maybe in the course of the afternoon she'd spot something that would make it all clear, some feature in Cindy notably lacking in herself. Youth and cuteness didn't seem enough to account for so much devastation. Cindy's hair was the color fortyish women often chose, somewhere between chestnut and gold, and there was a bit too much of it, Violet thought. She could also go easier on the makeup; the impression was altogether too bright, too much wattage. Violet ignored the half-spread arms and extended a hand. There were no prescribed words for this sort of meeting, but fortunately the dog made lots of noise. He was excited by the visitor and for no apparent reason seemed to take a shine to Violet.

"Come meet Lisa and Jenny." Obeying Cindy's wave, the teenage girls sidled up, more Seth's than their mother's, at least in appearance—lanky, olive-skinned, in tight jeans and bare midriffs. Nothing much to say. Well, what could they say? Their father's first wife? Opposite of a stepmother—a negative quantity, no word in the language for what she was to them. Could they even believe their father had once been married to her, a doctor, they'd surely been told, with shiny black hair gathered in a knot at her neck, green eyes—tiger eyes, Seth used to say—and of all things, a designer suit for a family dinner? Yet it was their admiration she would have liked, more than Cindy's. To her chagrin, Violet was wishing they could find her in every way more awesome and glamorous than their mother, unattainably glamorous. A futile wish, she knew, for their idea of glamour would be a bared navel studded with a rhinestone.

Drinks and snacks appeared. Five minutes later Grace was at the door, exuberant even after the four-hour drive from Boston, rushing over to Violet first. "Mom, it's so great to see you! I've missed you! I took two days off so I can stay with you."

Violet lapsed into easeful pleasure, a kind of melting from within. Her daughter brought a change of weather, light breaking through smog. Next came the guests of honor, the reason for this reunion: Evan, returning home after two years in Prague, with a wife, a new baby, and mounds of luggage. Her son had gone away a boy, she thought with a lump in her throat, and come back a man. Embraces, clamor, everyone happy and beautiful. So happy, so beautiful, that Violet was stunned to be feeling joy here in Seth's house. She could almost ignore Cindy's high-pitched, restless voice. In fact if Cindy and her sulky girls would be considerate enough to disappear, this would be her family, her loved ones assembled, blooming, thriving. She would have had time to watch Seth grow old and his decline would not be so appalling.

Not that she wanted him back. God, no. She was no longer the woman who could contort herself to fit his erratic moods. She just wanted to pretend, for one Sunday afternoon, that all the banal ugliness of his leaving had never taken place, the mutual rants, accusations, recriminations. And when they stopped, the dialogues that kept fomenting in her head, with her supplying Seth's half, brutally parsing her every failing, social, sexual, culinary, political, parental . . . until she'd exhausted her imagination. The whole ordeal was like some dreadful disaster cliché—earthquake, volcano, hurricane—and in the aftermath she had set about rebuilding. But so many disaster areas never regain their former luster.

After his bottle, the four-month-old baby was passed around. Violet could have swept him off to a private room and held him in her arms all day, but she didn't prolong her turn. There would be plenty of time to revel. She simply recorded the soft, compact feel of him, a memory to return to later, as she used to record the feel of Seth's caresses to summon up the next morning when her patients arrived with their woes, their cataracts, their ripped corneas and detached retinas.

When Seth's turn came he cradled the baby awkwardly, letting the head loll backward over the crook of his elbow as the small torso threatened to slip from his grasp. Violet held her breath.

"Not like that!" Cindy darted over to settle the bundle securely in his arms. "With Lisa and Jenny I was always afraid he'd drop them on their heads, he had such a weird way of holding them."

Seth shot a glance at Violet. His myopic eyes, narrowed behind the frameless octagonal glasses, were duller than she remembered. She used to write his prescriptions. He might need a change; he was squinting, though it could have been from anger. If she'd ever spoken that way in public, which was inconceivable, he would have been enraged. Anyway, he'd held their babies just fine.

The message in his face—unmistakably a message— was complex and would have to be decoded at leisure. But even this quick glance, like a glance at a patient, told something. Embarrassment, along with a cavalier disregard for it: we know each other so well, Violet, I can afford to let you see my embarrassment. Depletion. Maybe self-pity. All so unlike what she'd imagined. All these years, as she glided over the even surface of her life—her work, her succession of men, her friends—she'd pictured Seth as the doting husband and father, and as being doted on in turn, basking in fond attention. Years ago Violet would have loved the taste of this moment; now it soured her mouth.

Suddenly Seth began bouncing the baby in the air. Encased in its terry cloth, the child gurgled and giggled.

He's just been fed, Violet thought. If you keep that up he'll spit all over you.

She was prophetic. From the baby's lips, parted in glee, popped a gob of clotted milk that formed a spreading island on the front of Seth's blue shirt.

"Oh, I'm so sorry." Carla, the new daughter-in-law, rushed over with a wad of tissues, dabbing furiously at the shirt, then at the baby's glistening chin.

Cindy shook her head. "I had a feeling that would happen." She looked at Violet for confirmation: we mothers know, don't we? Violet couldn't bring herself to grin in complicity. She hadn't forgotten Grace and Evan's teenage reports on Cindy, offered along with the photos. Grace: She doesn't like me using her shampoos. She watches how I do the dishes. I tie up the phone too long. Evan: She says I'm a sloppy eater. She didn't want me taking the car . . . Violet had counseled patience. Soon they'd be grown and none of it would matter. For herself, though, long after she was able to think of Seth without anger, the shampoo and the forbidden car still rankled.

Cindy had barely spoken when Lisa and Jenny moaned in unison like a Greek chorus. "Yuck. You smell all cheesy, Dad."

More stooped than before, Seth trudged upstairs and reappeared in an old tan sweater. His sparse graying hair was slightly mussed like a boy's, as if his mother had tousled it affectionately. That must have happened when he pulled the sweater over his head and didn't think to repair the damage. He looked more boyish now—a boy afflicted by premature aging—than he had in his youth.

"Dinner!" Cindy announced brightly. Seth circled the table pouring wine (a less than steady hand, Violet noted—anxiety or Parkinson's?) while Cindy carried platters out from the kitchen. Be sure to say something, Violet reminded herself. Give credit where it's due. She probably couldn't have managed a dinner on such a grand scale. She was long out of the habit, just a meal now and then for a few women friends, or for Philip, her occasional lover of the past three years.

"Dad, you passed me by," Lisa, the fifteen-year-old, complained. "Don't I get any wine?"

"Well, I don't think . . ."

"Come on, it's a special occasion."

He poured her half an inch.

"Me too, then," wailed Jenny.

"Uh-uh. Thirteen is too young."

"What on earth are you doing?" said Cindy, entering with a bowl of rice. "Wine? You know it's not allowed. Lisa, put that down this minute. What is the matter with you, Seth?"

"A few drops won't do any harm."

"Well, I'm definitely old enough and I'd love some, Dad." That was Grace the good, extending her glass to salvage the moment. Seth didn't seem to hear her. He was staring at Violet again with some kind of appeal in his face. But what could she do? She couldn't even fix his rumpled hair.

"This roast beef is marvelous, Cindy. And the green rice. How do you do that?"

By sautéing it lightly first and using plenty of parsley,

Cindy disclosed. She'd be glad to share the recipe. It was the least she could do, thought Violet, and leaned down to stroke the dog, who'd parked himself beside her chair.

What was Seth appealing for? Rescue? He must know it was too late for rescue. They were both too sensible, too adult—too old!—for any impulsive return of the prodigal husband. An appeal nonetheless. For pity? Forgiveness? She could hardly even muster regret anymore. There was just the desiccation of the postvolcanic terrain.

"So, Evan, tell us about Prague." Grace again, determined to keep the chatter going. "It's not still the new Paris, is it? Was it ever, really?"

Well, yes, it had quieted down, he told them, but they should have seen it a couple of years ago . . . "We were constantly meeting people we knew on the streets. If you can't make it in New York, try Prague. That was the mantra." He turned to his half-sisters. "We got some really good stuff coming through for a while. The Orient Express. The Original Oregano Head Trip."

"The Orient Express?" said Seth. "I thought they discontinued that. And what the hell is the Original Oregano—whatever?"

Oh, stop, Violet urged mutely. Keep still and wait.

"They're groups, Dad," said Lisa with a contempt made sharper by its restraint. Seth's pouring her the wine evidently hadn't won him any points. Jenny tittered, and both girls rolled their eyes.

"Oh. Groups," he echoed uncertainly.

Everyone but Violet burst out laughing. Carla clapped her hand over her mouth and looked around for guidance: is it okay to laugh? Even the dog barked with what seemed like amusement, and again Violet stroked it. In his confusion Seth was gazing at Violet.

"You know, rock bands," she murmured.

"Oh, right." He smiled wanly, trying to join in the merriment, but it was too late.

"By the way, Dad," Evan said, "you'll like this. I used to see Vaclav Havel sometimes in one of the local cafés. People just went right up and spoke to him."

Seth had admired Havel from the time he was a dissident playwright in blue jeans. Speak up, Violet beamed in Seth's direction. Take your rightful place. But he just nodded and bent absorbedly over his plate. Food, she'd learned way back in her internship, is the last best pleasure of the old.

There wasn't much lingering after the fruit salad. Lisa and Jenny vanished and pounding music came from upstairs. Carla excused herself to tend to the baby. Evan went out to admire Grace's new car while Seth helped Violet on with her coat. He'd always done that, even though she would have preferred to do it herself. But she was too civil to rebuff any well-meant impulse. How careful she'd been, in so many ways, and what had it gotten her? Cindy wasn't careful. Cindy had a free hand. Seth wasn't going anywhere, surely not now. And Cindy was fed up. Her prosperous, sexy wheeler-dealer would soon be retiring, doddering around the house day and night, underfoot. More trouble than the dog. Who would have dreamed she could be the instrument of the revenge Violet once craved. No, be kind to him, Violet wanted to tell her in farewell, but that would never do. She might have said it to the girls—she no longer cared what they thought of her—but that would only make things worse.

He gave her the look again as she said goodbye. This time his face was overlaid with misery. Regret. She would have been patient, the look said. He wouldn't have been the butt of jokes, with her. She would have been gracious, indulgent with his mishaps, keeping him well informed. Those were the rewards a faithful husband reaps after a lifetime of decent behavior. And now . . .

But you would have had to tolerate me, Violet thought, and you didn't love me. She'd wasted hours pondering why she'd become unloved and still didn't know; maybe no one ever did. All she knew was that he couldn't give up his bliss in those solid pink arms.

Those pink arms were clasping the dog, as Cindy knelt down in a lavish spasm of affection that was also a restraining embrace, so the eager creature wouldn't leap on Violet to protest her leaving. "Kootchy kootchy poochy-woochy," Cindy kept repeating in little-girl squeals, letting the dog lick her face till it shone.

That was how it must have been, kootchy kootchy, pink and smoochy. That was what he had craved and bought at so high a price. For that she had had to suffer. It was no more just or rational than the arbitrary blows of disease, the failures of vision she dealt with every day, and it could hardly be called a surprise. Even the devastation and the calm aftermath seemed inevitable now, the detachment hollowed out inside her like a crater. And yet seeing it so clearly brought a jolt.

She tried to telegraph back the kindly message he wanted: I'm sorry it turned out this way. I would help you if I could. But as the door shut behind her, her face showed envy, not sorrow. He owned all the misery his risks had earned; he was in the thicket of his mistakes, impaled, fending off an excess of feeling, even if it was remorse. His life was dense and palpitating. She was clean and dry as old bones.

Faux-Me

I'd had enough. Enough of her intrusions, her comments and contradictions, making me feel that whatever I was doing should be done differently, or possibly not at all. She had opinions on everything, my work, my tastes and habits, and didn't hesitate to express them. Even when she was silent I could sense her disapproval. The other day she criticized my cooking, of all things. I don't cook a lot, it's just me since my daughter left for college, but now and then I pull myself together and try to eat properly. Faux-Me said I'd overcooked the chicken. True, I forgot about it in the oven while I was practicing, but it still tasted okay, more or less.

All that in addition to the rock band that moved in upstairs had pushed me to my limit. So finally I told her, "Look, if you think you can do better, why don't you take over for a day? You think it's easy juggling everything?"

I didn't really mean it, it was one of those impulsive remarks that pop out when you're irritated, but Faux-Me agreed with enthusiasm. "Great," she said. "I thought you'd never ask. Tomorrow, okay?"

Since I had offered, I couldn't say no. I hate to go back on my word; I even hate breaking dates. Faux-Me found my scruples laughable. "Give yourself a break, why don't you?"

she'd say. "It's not like anyone's keeping score." Odd she should say that, because I did have a half-submerged sense of being called to account for everything I did. In weak moments I could be assailed by fantasies of being on the witness stand and made to justify my most trivial actions. *Can you tell the court why you decided to take the bus and not the train? Or why you returned your library books late when you pass the library every day? I know this sounds absurd but you can't control your fantasies, can you?*

It was a few months after my husband's death in Iraq that Faux-Me started showing up. The worst possible time. I was already shaky, I didn't need her questioning my every move. He was a reporter for a national magazine and his hotel was blown up. Collateral damage. I had a terrible feeling something like that would happen, and it did. We were young then, married for only five years, still immersed in love, and we had a four-year-old. We were thinking of another, so besides grieving over him I grieved over that baby, never even conceived. But now I'm glad. It's been hard enough with one. I don't know how I would have managed with two.

I'm supposed to be working on a Ph.D. thesis in musicology. Plus I play the viola with a new chamber quartet, close friends from Juilliard. So far we've done mainly local schools, churches, small theaters. One of our performances got a short review in *New York Magazine*: "a spirited, up-and-coming new group." So we're hopeful. Still, the money is negligible, so I teach kids at an after-school program. That in addition to my thesis, which is on an obscure Italian eighteenth-century composer suggested by my adviser, makes for a struggle.

The new upstairs neighbors arrived a couple of weeks ago, three brothers from Guatemala, a successful rock band in their native country. They're looking for gigs here but they need a singer, as well as some contacts. This they told me in stumbling English the first time I went upstairs to ask them politely to please limit their playing to reasonable hours.

Each time I went up the music would stop for a while, then start again early the next day. It was hard to be angry with them: they were nice guys, very friendly, always offered me coffee and some delicious Guatemalan treat I never got the name of. So I'd wind up sitting down and chatting. I explained it's not that I don't like music, I'm a musician myself. And they sounded great. It was simply the crazy hours they rehearsed.

The band was already going when the alarm rang at seven-thirty, the morning after I lost my cool with Faux-Me. She reached out to shut it off and rolled over again. I protested but she reminded me it was her day to take charge.

"Another half-hour or so in bed won't matter," Faux-Me said. "It's not one of your teaching days." So we snuggled back under the covers.

"How can I sleep with that racket upstairs?"

"You're the one who won't call the landlord, so don't complain to me."

Faux-Me wanted me to stick up for my rights and tell the landlord. But I was reluctant to report them. From what Felipe, the drummer, said, I suspected they were illegal immigrants who had somehow slipped across the border. He told me they'd started out with their sister, who was their singer, but she died on the trip. I imagined her dying from suffocation, locked in an airless van. Notifying the landlord might bring in the law and in the current climate they could be deported back to Guatemala and who knows what awful conditions. I'd rather endure the noise than ruin their future.

"Anyhow," Faux-Me murmured as I pressed the pillow over my head, "you don't have to be anywhere till lunch."

"Lunch? What lunch?"

"I made a date with Rita. We haven't seen her in such a long time. We're meeting her at one in a Middle Eastern place around Lincoln Center."

She must have done this last night as I was falling asleep over my email. I had absolutely no memory of writing to Rita, but Faux-Me clearly had taken advantage of my lapse. I rarely make lunch dates; I don't like to break up the work-day. But Rita was a dear friend and I couldn't hurt her feelings by backing out now.

After a while I got up and made some coffee, then phoned the dentist for an appointment; he kept sending me reminders. The next thing I knew, Faux-Me snatched the phone. "Hey," I cried. "I've got things to take care of. Besides the dentist, the cleaners about my zipper, the cable TV people about the bill. And my email."

"That can all wait until tomorrow. There's always to-morrow," she said slyly. This was one of our long-standing conflicts. Her m.o., as I well knew by now, was never do to-day what you can put off until tomorrow. "And you checked your email late last night. What could have happened since then?"

"I don't know. Maybe Candace needs something." My daughter, in her first semester of college, seemed to be ad-justing well. I've heard some kids call and text their parents obsessively during that first term, but she barely calls once a week, usually sounding rushed.

"Cut the crap," said Faux-Me. "I know what you're wait-ing for. A message from Mr. Not Quite Right."

She had me there. Larry was away at some business conference, or so he said, and hadn't gotten in touch for days. Faux-Me, needless to say, didn't like Larry. She hadn't liked any man I'd dated over the years, not that there've been many. I wasn't smitten by any of them myself, but they do relieve the loneliness, at least for a while. Faux-Me claims to have higher standards, and she can tolerate being alone. "Do you want to get like your friend April?" she would taunt me. "She sleeps with men we wouldn't have coffee with." Some of her objections to Larry were valid, I admit. But I wasn't ready to end it altogether. It had only been four months. It was still worth it, just for someone halfway decent to spend the night with, when our schedules worked out.

Since I'd put Faux-Me in charge for the day, I gave in on the email—there was probably nothing from Larry anyway—and opened up the file with my research notes. I tried to focus on the obscure eighteenth-century Italian composer, but besides the music from upstairs, my mind kept drifting to trivia like I should really call a plumber about that drip in the bathtub, but the old plumber I liked had moved to Florida. When I began the research Faux-Me warned that I'd get tired of it pretty soon. But my adviser was pushing this topic.

"Stand up to her," Faux-Me urged. "Otherwise you'll be bored for two years. Why not a contemporary woman composer?" Lately it seemed she might be right. The more I studied the obscure Italian's music, the more I felt his obscurity had been earned.

But it was a serious commitment. My adviser might think I was flighty and could give me a hard time. So I kept on. That was me.

"I know what," Faux-Me interrupted as she saw me beginning to nod. "Let's put that away for now and practice for the concert coming up."

"Really? Right now?"

"Right now."

As soon as I had the viola tucked under my chin I started to feel better. We were doing one of the late Haydn string quartets. All thoughts of the plumber and the dentist fell away. Real time receded and was replaced by the tempo of the music. My ear conjured up the other strings around me and I paused for their parts.

Suddenly I put the instrument down. I couldn't go on. A brief passage in the piece sounded like "Norwegian Wood" and reminded me of a game my husband and I used to play in bed long ago, singing snatches of popular tunes and seeing if we could remember all the words. I thought of how I could never do anything like that with Larry, who was not a game-playing sort. He worked in finance, doing I couldn't figure out what.

"Have some more coffee and keep going. You only stopped because you're feeling sorry for yourself again."

Usually I could take Faux-Me's comments in stride—after all this time I'd gotten used to them. But every once in a while her words dived deep and sent my feelings roiling like the wake of a ship. I couldn't resort to the usual bickering. I sat down without a word.

"All right, never mind," she said. "Forget the music for now. It's time to get ready to meet Rita anyway." I obeyed and slunk off.

But after that brief moment when she relented, she started in again in the shower—it was one of her favorite places to pester me.

"As for that creep, you know he's seeing someone else. What do you need him for?"

That was true. Aside from a couple of broken dates recently—urgent work matters, he said—I'd spotted him last week with a tall red-haired woman, waiting in line for a George Clooney movie he knew I wanted to see. George Clooney reminds me of my late husband, who was almost as good-looking but didn't have the gray hair, more a kind of light coffee color. I scooted past the movie line, hoping he hadn't noticed me. No point in mentioning it. He'd say she was his cousin visiting from out of town, something like that. Faux-Me's question, what did I need him for, was harder to answer. And what did he need me for?

"I've got to get dressed," I snapped. "Can we discuss this later?"

"Okay, make it quick. It's too beautiful a day to stay inside."

Indeed, my window, facing east, was filled with a blazing October blue. "It's not even a weekend, you know," I said.

"So what? Is there some law that you can only enjoy yourself on the weekend? Besides, you often spend half of Saturday doing laundry or in the supermarket."

She was certainly on the mark today. I was "keeping busy," as everyone advised when it first happened. It wasn't hard to do—I really was busy. Yet I always had the sense that I wasn't accomplishing enough. How much was enough? I was possessed by some elusive standard of "enough" that I never managed to meet, like Zeno's arrow. This issue sometimes came up at my imaginary court appearances.

Faux-Me blithely hailed a taxi to go downtown. She loathed the subway, as I well knew.

Rita was diverting as usual, especially on the subject of the men in her real-estate office, whom she compared to characters in that painful David Mamet play. She noticed that I ordered the cassoulet as opposed to my usual salad, and also that I had dessert, key lime pie.

"No more diet?" she teased. Rita is slightly plump and seems contented that way. Her husband is plump too so I guess that makes it okay.

"I'm taking a day off in honor of seeing you," I said. "Who knows what would happen if I indulged like this all the time?"

"Only one way to find out."

After we parted, with the usual promise to meet again soon, Faux-Me led me to the Gauguin show at the Metropolitan Museum. Contemplating the languid, half-naked women with their sleek long hair and serene faces made me want to give up everything and move to Tahiti at once. But of course Tahiti today is probably filled with people talking on cell phones, and I don't suppose the women go around in sarongs anymore. Thinking of cell phones, I realized mine had not rung all day. I reached into my purse to check for messages.

"Uh-uh," said Faux-Me. "I turned it off."

I didn't even attempt to argue. There was something soothing about her brusque commands, relief of a sort. We walked across Central Park in the balmy early fall weather, stopping for ice cream. I wondered if the Guatemalan brothers upstairs lived like this, strolling about enjoying the sunshine. They didn't seem to have any regular employment. How did they manage to pay the rent? Faux-Me suspected they might be drug dealers, but I wouldn't accept her bigotry. They were nice young men and aside from the blaring music I had no objection to them as neighbors.

Next stop was the gym, where I hadn't been for so long that my membership had expired. Faux-Me whipped out a credit card to renew and chatted with the girl at the desk. After some time on the weight machines and the treadmill, watching old sitcoms on the overhead TV, she said, "Now, didn't that feel good?"

"Oh, quit being so patronizing," I muttered. But she was right, as she had often been over the years.

When at last we returned home the upstairs music was blaring, but I was in a good mood after the minivacation so I tolerated it. Hours later, however, my kindly feelings started to change. They were still going strong at midnight. Why should I have to endure this? I had work; I needed my sleep. If they wanted to live here they should be considerate of their neighbors. I put on a robe and went upstairs to knock on the door. I said I couldn't take it anymore and if this kept up I'd have to call the landlord. Felipe looked stricken and was very apologetic. They had an audition tomorrow and were nervous about it. But of course they'd stop immediately.

To my surprise, Faux-Me seemed disturbed. "You don't really want to have them deported, do you?"

"No, but I also need my sleep. It's not fair."

She hesitated. "Well, it's a matter of degree, isn't it? I mean, your losing sleep compared to their getting sent back to who knows what kind of life. They've already lost a sister."

"I can't believe this. You've changed your mind?"

"You've already had your life wrecked by violence. Do you want to inflict that on others?"

It was another of those knife-blade moments when I couldn't hurl back a cutting reply. We were both silent.

Since I was too worked up to sleep, I decided to catch up on my email and maybe go back to my research notes. I dashed off a few messages but really I was too upset to concentrate. I was angry not only at the guys upstairs, but also at Larry and the eighteenth-century Italian composer and my adviser, and life in general, and why didn't Candace ever call? All this swirled around in my head and before I knew it I was drowsing over the computer and eventually stumbled to bed.

Thankfully, it was quiet when I woke the next morning. Again Faux-Me turned off the alarm and tried to snuggle under the covers but this time I was firm. "You had your day," I said. "Now it's back to business as usual."

"Who ever decreed that you were in charge permanently? I have as much right to make decisions about our life as you do," she shot back.

"What are you talking about? I'm me! You're the faux one. You're the one who turns up just to make trouble."

"Make trouble? On the contrary. Do you really not get that? Don't forget, I could be you as easily as you can."

"So you say. Now shut up and let me get on with it."

That must have worked, because I didn't hear a peep for some time. I took the phone and a cup of coffee to my desk and found a text from Candace: "I'm sorry about not calling. You sound upset but please don't be. It's so hectic here, so much to get used to, but everything is going great and I met a guy and I'll call as soon as I have a minute. Love you!" At least somebody did.

Had I texted her to say I was worried? Apparently.

Next I found an email from Larry. He agreed with what I had written late last night, that maybe it would be best if we stopped seeing each other. I was a wonderful person and it wasn't my fault that things weren't working out. I had no memory of writing him. But there it was in my Sent folder, a curt note proposing we say adios. Faux-Me must have done all this while I was half asleep.

I was hardly surprised when I found my research notes had disappeared. They weren't in the trash or anywhere else when I did a search—she'd been quite thorough. I should have been furious with her, but frankly what I felt was relief. She'd simplified my life with a few clicks. If only she'd find a plumber and call the cable TV people as well. But that sort of thing didn't interest her.

"Don't pretend to throw a fit." She was back. "I know you're glad. You can't hide anything from me. After all, we're in this together."

What bothered me more was how she'd changed her mind about reporting the guys upstairs to the landlord. We'd switched places on that. Though now that it was quiet, I wasn't sure which side I was on anymore.

If she could morph into me, where did that leave me?

It occurred to me that I might allow Faux-Me to take charge indefinitely, or rather, I might continue my life as Faux-Me, indulging myself, trusting Candace though I missed her, taking time to walk through the park, and all the rest . . . After all, I knew Faux-Me as well as I knew myself. I—or should I say she?—could pose as me, using my body, my voice. In time it would cease to be a performance and would become me. For all I knew, many people—most people? all?—went about pretending to be other than what they were, pretending so well that they became the pretense.

Could I manage without Faux-Me? Or would I, the person who up to now I thought I was, become a Faux-Me? She—or should I say I?—would urge me to get up when the alarm clock rang, would try to curb my impulses and get down to work, would scold me for eating key lime pie followed by ice cream in the park . . .

As I mused in this way, I realized that Faux-Me had barely spoken for a good while. I missed her. She was not the same kind of company as a halfway decent man in bed, but she was company nonetheless. The unaccustomed quiet settled around me.

But not for long. Very soon it was broken by the pounding of drums and the heartfelt whir of guitars. It was after nine by now, but still . . . A flicker of anger rose in me, like a match struck. An instant later the trembling glow died, as it does when a match is flawed and can't sustain its flame.

Breaking Up

I'd barely picked up and said hello when the voice on the other end announced, "I'm breaking up with you." Harsh, angry.

"Who is this?" I asked. "I think you have the wrong number."

"Don't get smart with me. I know very well who I'm talking to. I told you, I'm breaking up with you."

She was so fiercely insistent, desperate, it seemed. I trembled.

"I told you, you have the wrong number. I don't even know you."

"Well, I know you. And don't try to talk me out of it. It's over. I'm breaking up with you."

It could be a child at play, the way we played as kids, bunched round the phone, calling all the funeral parlors in the book to say, "I'm dying to give you my business." Then we'd hang up fast, afraid of what they might reply but reveling in our boldness, bursting with laughter.

"Don't you hear? I'm breaking up with you," she repeated. "Stop pretending you don't know me." Obviously dying for a response.

This was no child, the voice was older. Thick with intensity, wild with rage. I hung up still trembling. Yet I was sorry for her too. I could tell she'd done it this way because she was afraid to do it face to face, afraid to be talked out of her determination. Or else she wanted to be talked out of it, in one of those protracted and agonizing dialogues that after close analysis of recent behavior would end in a reconciliation, each one promising to do better in the future.

Well, it was none of my concern, just a wrong number. But for days her voice and her words shadowed me. She spoke with such conviction. Had I forgotten someone? Who, who, who was it breaking up with me?

Intolerance

There was once a woman, a cabaret singer, who wanted very badly to have a baby. She felt stabs of longing when she saw infants in the arms of her friends, or being pushed in their strollers by tired-looking young women with short skirts and unkempt hair. The infants asleep with their mouths open looked cherubic, like creatures floating through the clouds of Renaissance paintings. She knew they didn't always sleep so amiably, that they required a lot of attention, but she wouldn't mind that. She could afford help. She could sing to the baby and it would love her. She needed someone to love her.

Her attempts at loving and being loved had not thus far been successful. She had been married twice, both times for short periods. Each time there had been something about the men, some quality she found intolerable. With one it had been his perpetual lateness, with the other an intimate habit she didn't care to recall. She was a fastidious woman who had great difficulty tolerating imperfection. In her singing she strove for perfection and sometimes thought she had attained it. When she fell short of her standards she was merciless in her self-castigation. Her most prized review was one in which the critic had called her rendition of certain songs "perfection itself."

But newborn babies, provided they were normal and

healthy, did seem perfect. It was only later that they developed the ordinary human imperfections she found so hard to bear. Ideally a baby would remain an infant forever, though alas that could never be. Still, she hoped that in time, she would continue to love the baby whatever its flaws. And the baby, uncritical as it would be, would love her. Babies love their mothers unless they are mistreated or abused in some way, and she would never mistreat a child.

She got pregnant easily with the help of a cooperative friend, who didn't want any fatherhood duties later on, which pleased her. It was to be her baby alone. The pregnancy, and even more so the birth, was arduous and offended her fastidiousness in many ways, but she bore these physical offenses as best she could, seeing as they were unavoidable if one wished to obtain a baby.

The baby, a girl, was pretty and winning just as she'd hoped. The only trouble was its crying. She knew infants cry a lot. But this baby had a particularly piercing cry that assailed her musician's ears. It was way in the upper registers of the human range, a very high "EEEEEE" that woke her from sleep and shot adrenalin through her, and her heart pounded fiercely long afterwards. She did everything she could to soothe the baby, changed her, rocked her, fed her, until she calmed down. But more and more she dreaded that cry, higher and shriller than any baby she had ever heard. Even after it stopped it vibrated in her head. In short, it was intolerable.

She did her best to tolerate it, though, hoping that as the baby grew, the cry would diminish in pitch and duration. This did not happen. The baby did cry less over time—she was well cared for, all her needs attended to—but when she did cry, it was that same unearthly sound. The doctor said there was nothing at all wrong, she was a healthy, sturdy baby. A relief, to be sure. But her relief did not ease the agony of the screeching.

Distraught, she dreaded that in a rash moment she might lose control and harm the child. She had frightful dreams about babies. Once she put a baby, who in the dream was very small, in an ice-cube tray and left it in the freezer. When she went to get ice cubes for a drink, she discovered the baby frozen solid, but still pink-cheeked. In other dreams, friends left her their pets in her care: one night it was a dog, another night a cat, another night a pair of hamsters, and she forgot to feed them, even forgot they were there. When the friends came to collect them they found the pets somewhere on the floor, stiff and cold, emaciated.

When she had rehearsals or performances she hired babysitters, neighborhood teenagers. Later she would ask if the baby had woken or cried. "Yes, she needed to be changed. She has a pretty powerful pair of lungs," they said, or words to that effect. But they said it lightly, even admiringly; clearly they were not bothered by the screeching sound.

Soon the baby became a toddler. She began to talk at the proper time and made the appropriate progress. In most ways she was charming and cried only when she had a reason. But to the woman's horror the baby's speaking voice was in that same upper register, a high-pitched squeak that sent chills up her spine like chalk on a blackboard. Of all the possible flaws a small child might have, this was the one that she simply could not tolerate.

With regret, she decided the best solution was to give the baby away. At least for a while. She appealed to her mother. Her mother was in late middle age, quite hale and capable of taking care of a baby. Moreover she was widowed, lonely, and not the least bit musical or sensitive to sounds, so the baby's shrill voice would not disturb her. Her mother accepted the baby willingly, though she made it clear that she strongly disapproved of her daughter's action. It was unnatural, she said. You don't give a baby away, especially such a lovely baby, just because you don't like its voice, she chided. There was no way to explain to her mother how the voice shattered her equilibrium.

Since the baby's birth she had dated several men, always hoping for one who could be a permanent companion. But she had sent them all away: in spite of their virtues each one had some trait or habit she found intolerable. One picked his nose in his sleep. Another left damp hair around the bathtub drain. Another had a slight stammer. Another had an eye that turned in.

She visited the baby—now attending preschool—at her mother's as often as she could. The child was thriving, a bright, cheerful girl who had adapted well to her new home. At her mother's house the child's voice did not sound quite as screechy—high-pitched but not intolerable. Maybe the voice was changing, she thought, and she took the little girl home for a few days. But as soon as the child was with her, the voice reverted to that ungodly shriek, and she had to bring her back to her mother's.

She still wanted a baby who could live with her and love her exclusively. But rather than endure the insults of another pregnancy and delivery, she decided to adopt a baby. This took some time, and during the wait she met a man who came to live with her, a man she was beginning to love, a man whose fatal flaw had not yet revealed itself. After a while she was the mother of another adorable infant girl, and the three made a small family. At first all went well—no shrieking, as she had unreasonably feared—but when it was time for the baby to start speaking, she didn't. The doctor assured her this was normal delayed speech, but when at last the baby spoke, her words were garbled. Tests showed that she was partially deaf. Only partially, the doctor said, and in a short while she could get cochlear implants, which would enable her to hear almost normally; eventually her speech would be normal as well. Otherwise she was a healthy, sturdy baby. Still, this imperfection galled the woman; she had hoped for a musical child.

She brought this baby to her mother as well, who accepted her gladly and didn't take the flaw at all seriously; she would arrange for the implants at the proper time. The man, who had grown to love the baby though he had no legal rights as father, tried to dissuade her from giving it away. In fact, he was grief-stricken. Like her mother, he felt the woman was behaving unnaturally, and to her astonishment he ended their relationship.

She had no intention of trying any more babies, and perhaps no more men either. Everyone she had tried to love so far—except that final man, who doubtless would soon have shown his intolerable flaw—was too imperfect. She finally went to a psychiatrist to find out why she couldn't love and be loved, and he, being a fatherly psychiatrist, explained patiently, as if to an ignorant child, that human beings were inherently flawed creatures and must be accepted as such.

Of course, she knew that already—everybody knew it—and so she was irritated by his explanation. It was far too simplistic; it didn't touch the root of her problem. There was something more, something obscure, buried deep in her. Why could she not accept imperfection?

In any case, his fatherly advice revealed his lack of professionalism, a serious flaw, and so she left abruptly, and resigned herself to a life of solitude. Of course, she herself, whom she must live with, was imperfect in many ways, but there was nothing she could do about that. Except destroy herself, but that would show a greater weakness than she could tolerate.

But I Digress . . .

I met a Russian at a party, a large jovial man with a broad
face, wearing a gray suit that looked heavily padded. Or
maybe the man himself was padded. He had attractively
messy fair hair and in one beefy hand he held a drink. Not
vodka, one of the amber ones. He was saying that nowadays
Moscow or St. Petersburg were much more desirable places
to live than New York, but since he had been here for twenty years and needed to attend to his thriving medical practice, what could he do? New York is ruined, he said. Too
many people. All kinds of people. In the winter he went to
Florida, some beach or other, to hang out with fellow Russians in the same predicament, too successful to return.

I suggested that if he wanted to see Russians near a
beach he had only to go to Brighton Beach in Brooklyn.

He said, Oh no, those are not really Russians.

No? I said. Hmm. They appeared to be Russian. They
spoke Russian. They had colonized the neighborhood: all
the signs were in Russian, the streets were lined with Russian
restaurants and stores selling Russian food. When I walked
along the boardwalk and saw the stocky people swaddled
in their heavy coats against the wind coming off the ocean,
the women with their hair dyed yellow or orange like my
mother's, sitting on benches gossiping, the men striding
along with their bellies leading and gesticulating with the
hand that held their big glowing cigars like my father's, I

was seeing my old aunts and uncles, my father's brothers and sisters. Except my aunts and uncles had arrived decades earlier and so had learned to look and sound and dress like Americans. But they probably looked like that once. Now most of them were dead.

The Russian shook his head. When I speak Russian to those people, he said, they don't really understand. They speak a different Russian. They're not really Russians.

My father never spoke about his childhood in Russia, now Ukraine. I couldn't get a thing out of him. Not that I really tried. It was as if it had never happened, or it had happened but was not fit for the ears of children, like a visit to a brothel or something of which one is secretly ashamed. Once I referred to my father's background as Russian. He corrected me. "Being Jewish in Russia," he said, "is not being Russian." Then what is it? I wondered. But I didn't ask. Another time when I happened to mention the name of Vladimir Lenin, in relation to some school assignment, he corrected my pronunciation: not "*Vlad*imir" but "Vla*di*mir." I was embarrassed and never made that mistake again, not that Lenin's given name was one I had many occasions to utter. That was the only time my father indicated that he knew or had known Russian.

My father's next older brother, George, had a different attitude. I once met him on the New York subway and was surprised to learn that he was on his way to a course in Russian at The New School in Greenwich Village. He wanted to "brush up."

I don't know if my mother knew much about my father's childhood, whether it was the kind of thing he talked about when they met and were courting. One thing she did tell me: he would never eat a banana because it was not something he had ever seen as a boy. Perhaps an orange too. What an odd thing to avoid, an innocent, bland banana, as if it were something like escargots or fried locusts. Of course, the latter are not generally available in the New World.

The only other clue that my father had had a Russian childhood was that he often quoted Lenin's saying, "Religion is the opiate of the people." Though strictly speaking, a Russian childhood is not required for someone to quote those words. Now that I think of it, it wasn't Lenin who said that but Karl Marx, a German Jew. Those people at Brighton Beach, I told the man at the party, they're Russian Jews.

Everyone knew this. We could remember that they arrived in the 1970s when Russia relaxed its policies towards Jews and allowed them to leave; some went to Israel and some came to Brighton Beach, where I had learned to swim as a child, now known as Little Odessa. I had a friend who ran an agency that found jobs for the many Russian doctors, lawyers, and so on, who could find work only as janitors or dishwashers. She would tell me their stories, immigrant stories; their expectations. They were disappointed. They had expected a welfare state and now they had to fend for themselves. They came as doctors and became janitors. The Russian doctor I met at the party, I deduced, never went through the janitor phase; he was post-1989. My father didn't get very excited over the Jews coming because he had no relatives left to come. The older brother they had left there some sixty years before was no doubt dead with his family, possibly tossed in the ditch at Babi Yar.

That's right, said the Russian doctor at the party, nodding.

So you mean they're not ethnic Russians. Is that what you mean?

Yes, he said.

Even though he had been in America for twenty years and boasted of his thriving medical practice, which was why he couldn't return to Moscow or St. Petersburg as he would have preferred, he hadn't yet learned that at a cocktail party in certain parts of New York City one doesn't talk about people being or not being ethnically this or that. I didn't enlighten him. Let him keep it up. Let someone else catch him on it one day.

The Russian doctor at the party was reawakening scenes with my father, especially his last weeks when he lay in a condition described as a stupor. Less than a coma but more than a sleep. He had lain in this state for days and I was impatient to have it be over, to have him either wake up or die. He would hate to be seen lying there looking dead, with tubes emerging from under the blankets carrying his bodily emissions and emptying them into large jars on the floor under the bed. After a few days of this I asked his doctor if my father was in a coma and, if so, how long it could be expected to last. The doctor said, I'd call it a stupor. About how long it might last, he gave me a condescending look and said he couldn't answer those kinds of questions. I didn't mistake you for God, I replied. I just wanted your opinion as a doctor.

One of my father's four older sisters, Frieda, came to the hospital to visit him. She lived in Far Rockaway, near the ocean. It was a long trip for her; the hospital was in Lower Manhattan. The subway was difficult, a cab was unlikely ... Maybe someone gave her a ride. By some means, she appeared, or rather was heard first, clicking down the hall. She was a small old bony woman with fierce energy whose features exuded a formidable will. She spoke with authority, as had all of my aunts and uncles. She was one of the few remaining.

My father was the youngest of nine children, their ages like steps, about a year and a half between each birth. Considering that most of them were in their teens or early twenties when they came to America, from a town near Kiev where they spoke Yiddish at home and Russian in school, their command of English was remarkable. I don't mean simply that they were fluent. They spoke in gorgeously folded sentences, origami-like sentences, the way characters do in Victorian novels. My father, who was eleven or twelve when he arrived, spoke perfect, unaccented English. He acquired a large vocabulary and used many distinctive and rich words not in common use by the native-born: "manifest" and "belligerent" were among his favorites. George, a year and a half older, the one who was studying Russian, had the barest trace of an accent, and so on up for the rest. They were a family talented at languages; hearing them speak, following the arabesques of their sentences, was a pleasure regardless of the slight accent of the oldest ones, a pleasure maybe even enhanced by the accent.

Aunt Frieda had very large teeth that seemed to share in the formation of her words. She had reddish brown hair pulled back in an upsweep, a word and style one doesn't hear or see much anymore. She was one of the middle children; her speech was distinguished not so much by the accent as by a rare melodic lilt that might have come from the Middle East or one of the more remote regions of Asia. I noticed this Asian or Levantine quality also in my Aunt Anna and Uncle Dan, not in their speech but in their appearance, the broad foreheads, the slightly slanted eyes, the sallow skin. I suspected that an ancestor had been raped, or to be optimistic, seduced, by an invader from the East.

Aunt Frieda, who did not share that Eastern look—she had a narrow face with hollowed cheeks—was a seamstress and had often made clothes for me when I was a child. I would stand in her tiny living room draped in something or other while she fussed around me with pins in her teeth. I was fond of her—in her brusque, uncompromising nature I saw something of a kindred spirit, but I was even more fond of her husband, Uncle Dave, very different temperamentally from my aunts and uncles by blood. Dave's accent was Eastern European mixed with British; on his escape from whatever doomed region he came from, he landed first in England, where he remained for a time before coming to the United States. The histories of all of these aunts and uncles, by blood or by marriage, were notably vague, and now that they are all dead, are likely to remain so. It was as if the past were not quite as real as the lives they began here, or were best cast off like shabby, no longer usable clothes.

Uncle Dave was different from my father's family. He loved poetry and could wiggle his big ears. I delighted in his whimsical conversation (my father's family had no sense of whimsy), delivered in a soft, gravelly voice and that partly British accent. In his stories the line between fact and fiction was blurred, the way I liked it and still do. I was in my twenties when he died. Aunt Frieda, knowing I was so fond of him, said I could come over and pick out a book from his library to keep. I chose Maimonides's *Guide for the Perplexed*. I had heard of it in college but didn't imagine anyone still really read it, even less owned it. I was enchanted by the title. Frieda took it off the shelf but before she handed it to me she leafed through it quickly. "We sometimes keep money in books," she said. I, too, keep money in books, so I was entirely sympathetic to her checking the book.

I still haven't read it, only leafed through it, but I do like having it on my shelf; it reminds me of Uncle Dave and I like to imagine I might read it one day. I think I can count on remaining perplexed, about my father and many other things. But who knows, perhaps the title is the best thing about it. I must remember that the charm of that word "perplexed" may be due to the translator rather than Maimonides himself. Whatever word Maimonides used in Hebrew or Greek, it was the translator who came up with "perplexed." A lesser translator might have written "confused" or "puzzled." I have on occasion kept money between its pages.

Unlike Dave, my father was not a poetry lover but he did go to high school and to law school (college in between was not required back then) and he often quoted a handful of lines that had evidently dug a permanent groove in his memory. "Full many a flower is born to blush unseen / and waste its fragrance on the desert air," from Thomas Gray's "An Elegy in a Country Churchyard" which he used when referring to certain girl cousins already in their mid-twenties and unmarried. Another favorite was "Fools rush in where angels fear to tread," from Pope's *Essay on Criticism*. This he had ample occasion to use since he considered most people fools, or at least not as intelligent as himself. I didn't know where these lines came from and simply accepted them as a sort of gospel. What a surprise to find them on the pages of my college textbooks.

But about Aunt Frieda's visit. Memory is so prone to digression. To sustain a logical or chronological sequence, we must keep dragging our minds off their natural course, like a cowboy tugging on a calf with a rope around its neck who wants to run off into the fields.

Still wearing her coat and hat, Frieda leaned over my father's bed, her face inches from his, and with the thumb and forefinger of her right hand, she separated the upper and lower lids of his right eye. It was as if he were a piece of property she owned, furniture, or a newly completed garment she was checking for flaws. My stomach lurched at this terrible invasion of privacy. Even the eye burst out in protest, "Don't do that!" I suppose it was I who shouted those words but it seemed at the time that I and my father's violated eye were one.

To peer into what was behind a closed eyelid was not only invasive but indecent, like lifting a sleeper's skirt to have a peek. Maybe Frieda thought he had already become a thing, that is, a corpse. I would never normally yell at her—I was respectful to my aunts and uncles. But she didn't seem to care that I had yelled. She did let go of the eyelid, but not until she had ascertained that she couldn't wake him that way. She must have known he was alive; we would have told her if he had died, though he might have looked exactly the same the first few hours. No, she was simply trying to wake him from his stupor.

A few weeks before my father went to the hospital that last time, Father's Day came along. I wanted to get him something but couldn't think what he could use, in his present state. I finally bought him a shirt. It was a beautiful shade of blue, somewhere between royal blue and navy blue, with a pattern like small polka dots but not exactly dots, more like little plus signs, though that isn't exactly it either. I knew he would probably never be able to wear the shirt but I didn't want to come "empty-handed"—a phrase I had often heard from my mother—so I brought the shirt. I felt foolish giving it to him since it was so obvious he would never wear it, but he accepted it graciously, though not without a touch of irony. As if to say, ah, children, we have to humor them.

He never did wear the shirt and some months later, when my widowed mother was moving into my older sister's house, I came over to help her organize things for the move. My mother had never spent a night alone in any of the places she and my father had lived, and so it was inevitable that she would move in with my older sister and her husband, who lived nearby. Going through a closet, I came across the still brand-new shirt and took it home. I hung it in my closet. I would have liked to wear it but it was much too broad in the shoulders so I told my husband he could wear it, which he did, a number of times. I was glad the shirt was getting some use, but I could never look at it without thinking of my father and how indulgently he accepted the shirt.

The last time I drove up to visit my father at home, shortly after the shirt episode, I found him lying fully dressed on the living room couch, which was upholstered in a white-and-gold pattern my mother had chosen. At that time, late in his life, my father was part owner of a furniture store, the source of the couch. He knew nothing about furniture, he was even color blind; by training and inclination he was an accountant and tax lawyer. I imagine the store was one of his last-ditch efforts to make a pile of money. The store was in Chinatown and most of the customers were Chinese, so he and his partner hired a Chinese man for the day-to-day operations while they handled the accounting end. Both he and the partner had individual accounting practices so they had little time to devote to the store. Eddie, the Chinese manager, was extremely gracious when members of our family came to the store, and from what we could tell, not knowing Chinese, he appeared to be gracious with the customers too. The store did well for a time—until my father discovered that Eddie had been siphoning off money for his personal use, which stunned us all since he was so charming. My father and his partner didn't press charges— perhaps Eddie repaid the money—but they let him go and hired someone less charming. Meanwhile my mother, indeed everyone in the family, chose whatever furniture we wanted from the store. I didn't care for the heavy, ornate furniture and chose the simplest things I could find: a small red lamp and a round white kitchen table with four red chairs. My father seemed hurt, as if this was a judgment on his taste, even though he had no part in choosing the merchandise. Eddie did that.

He lay on the white-and-gold-covered couch flat on his back. I went over to kiss him. He accepted my kiss with tolerance and then turned his face to the wall. I remember thinking that phrase because I had read it in a famous story by Ernest Hemingway. The character who knows his end is near (not through illness but imminent murder) turns his face to the wall. Perhaps all those who know they will soon die by whatever means turn their faces to the wall.

When I visited him in the hospital, I brought my embroidery. A few years earlier, when my daughter, then four years old, needed an eye operation, I acquired a small piece of embroidery made for cross-stitching and brought it to do while I waited during the operation. I didn't think I could concentrate on reading. The embroidery had flowers and the alphabet and a design of a house. As a child I had done these pieces of embroidery with my friends, patiently cross-stitching for hours but never finishing anything. While my daughter was anesthetized and being cut I did a small section of the embroidery, a few of the alphabet letters, using the same metal hoop I had used as a child.

Hospitals were different back then. I slept overnight on a cot near my daughter's bed, but late at night I sat in a small waiting room for parents who were sleeping over, and I smoked. It's unimaginable today that anyone would smoke in a hospital, but it was common then. I chatted with the other parents and nurses who came in to smoke as well. The operation was successful, and when we got home I put the embroidery away.

So each time my father went to the hospital during his final illness I brought the embroidery and got a good way into it, most of the alphabet and several flowers, but never finished it. I've used it for other operations in the family and I still have it, not yet completed.

My father did eventually wake up from what the doctor called his stupor. He didn't say much but at least he was awake and could understand what we said to him. He had excellent nurses caring for him, kind and deft. A blonde Midwesterner, one from the Philippines, and the night nurse, Eva, a Polish immigrant. They tried to speak to him, just casual pleasantries, but he wouldn't respond. When they were out of earshot he muttered, "You can't trust any of them." I was shocked because throughout his life he had had many non-Jewish clients, as well as a few friends. He couldn't mean it, I thought. It was a feeling from his secret childhood bubbling up to the surface like part of a drowned body that sometimes surfaces in a river. My first urge was to object. But with him so uncomfortable and near death, it was no time for a lecture on brotherhood. So I let it pass.

As things got worse he began making an odd motion that I found baffling. Perplexing, I should say. He put his thumb and the first two fingers of his right hand together and made a turning motion. I thought he wanted to write something and offered him a pencil. I was used to seeing him with a yellow number 2 pencil in his right hand, which he used for his accounting: big ledger books with columns of figures that he added in his head, running the sharp point of the pencil down the columns. But he shook his head—he didn't want the pencil. He kept making the motion and I never understood it.

Only after his death did it strike me what he was doing. He was asking us to turn off the switch and let him die. The only trouble was, he was not being kept alive by any switch, any artificial means, no ventilator or anything. His heart was very strong and simply wouldn't stop regardless of his readiness.

The heart did stop eventually. The day of his funeral was a sunny day in August and a lot of people attended. But that night came a heavy rain. All I could think of was that he was lying in the sodden earth. The earth of what was now his native land, because his first twelve years as a Jew in Russia were gone, practically speaking, except in his mind. It rained steadily and hard, and I had the almost uncontrollable desire to go to the cemetery and stand over his grave with an umbrella. I could finally ask him what it had been like in his childhood in Russia, a question I had never managed to ask. He would have disliked being asked and would not have answered. Maybe now, dead and sodden, he would have no reason to immerse those years in silence. He might have grown indifferent. Or if not indifferent, accepting.

Am I a Thief?

First things first: I have bad feet. Otherwise this entire incident would never have happened. I prefer not to go into details about the feet—they're rather intimate parts, don't you think? Witness foot fetishes, for example. Or the binding of women's feet in China, for which many cultural reasons have been adduced, but which always struck me as quite simple: women's feet were bound so that they couldn't run away. There may be cultures where bare feet aren't shown in public, like breasts in ours. A recent cover of a popular magazine showed a woman's mastectomy scar while her other, healthy, breast was covered. Curious that it was okay to display a bare if damaged chest on every newsstand in the land, but not an ordinary breast. But I digress.

My bad feet make it difficult to find comfortable shoes for walking, shoes that don't cause pain and yet are reasonably attractive. Believe me, I've searched, but with little success. That little success yields shoes that are broad, flat, rubber-soled, generally ugly, and hardly suitable for social occasions, which bothers me, perhaps more than it should, but so be it. Somewhere, in some remote shop or online catalogue there must be shoes of the kind I seek, but they elude me.

The incident I'm thinking of occurred in a half-deserted movie theater on a midweek afternoon. It was clearly not

a popular movie, at least not yet—an adaptation of an obscure nineteenth-century Spanish novel. I had been asked
to review it for a film magazine. I often go to the movies
alone in the afternoon for these assignments. I took off my
shoes, as I like to do in darkened theaters, and placed them
neatly under my seat. When the movie was over—quite
good, unexpectedly; I could write a positive review—I
poked my feet under the seat for my shoes. To my surprise
my toes dragged forth a different pair of shoes, not mine.
They were black leather with low thick cork heels and a narrow T-strap, and looked roomy but still simple and elegant.
Just the kind of shoes I wanted. I like a heel, as most women
do, because it gives a nice tilt to one's bearing. But whereas I
used to go everywhere in three- or four-inch heels, now I'm
limited to low ones. In the dark, while the credits began, I
slipped the shoes on. They fit perfectly and felt quite comfortable. Oddly enough I wasn't surprised. I had a feeling
they might fit, and perhaps were even left there on purpose
for me. Fate? I remembered the shoemaker's elves in the
fairy tale, though I am not generally of a whimsical turn of
mind.

A moment later I felt the woman in the seat behind
me rummaging under my seat. Whether she had taken
off her shoes because her feet hurt, I can't say; some people just like to go without shoes. Unlike me, she must have
leaned back—the movie house had those huge leather reclining seats—stretched out her legs and slipped her shoes
off beneath my seat. She gave a little "Oh" of surprise when
instead of her own pretty shoes she discovered my ugly
ones of stretchy canvas with rubber soles. The ads said they
would make you feel like you were walking on air, but they
did no such thing.

I could hear the woman fussing around nearby seats in

her row, no doubt to look under them. When we have lost something we tend to look in places it could not possibly be, maybe to postpone facing the unpleasant truth that the thing is gone. I was trying to get away as soon as I could, but I dropped my purse, which gave her a moment to tap me on the shoulder and ask politely if I would check under my seat—she'd lost her shoes. I had to comply. "I'm sorry, there's nothing there," I said in a low voice, because some people were still watching the lengthy credits, which I could look up online later for my review.

"This is the oddest thing," she whispered back. "I'm sure I left my shoes under there. Do you mind if I just come around and check?"

I couldn't get out since she was turning the corner of the rows and moving towards me. She lifted up every seat until she got to mine, and I edged aside so she could look. Meanwhile she held my shoes in one hand.

"I don't get it," she said. "Is it possible my shoes got mixed up with someone else's? Are these yours by any chance?" She held my ugly shoes away from her with some distaste.

"No, sorry. Excuse me," and I slid past her. But once I was in the aisle, she was right behind me and must have looked at my feet, because she cried out, "Those are my shoes! You've got my shoes on!"

"No," and I smiled sympathetically. "You must be mistaken. These are mine. I've had them for months."

"That's ridiculous," she snapped, regardless now of the people still watching the credits. "Don't you think I know my own shoes? Look, you must have made a mistake in the dark. Let's just exchange and forget the whole thing."

"I'm not taking off these shoes," I said firmly but civilly. "I came in with them and I'm leaving with them." I was

grateful at that moment that it was not a hat or scarf at issue, which she might tug away. There is no way to remove
shoes from a person who is standing in them.

"You're stealing my shoes," she said harshly. "I can't possibly wear these," and with a grimace she thrust my shoes
at me, but I refused to accept them. "I'm going to find the
manager."

"And say what?" I asked. "That I took your shoes? He'll
think you're crazy. Who steals shoes in a movie?"

We were now almost at the lighted lobby and I could
see her clearly for the first time. She was about my age and
height and had the same straight glossy dirty-blonde hair
pulled back in a barrette at her neck. Our resemblance was
uncanny—like me, she was good-looking if not quite beautiful, in a simple, classic way. She was dressed as I was too,
in tailored slacks and a silk shirt tucked in. I was dressed
that way because I'd had lunch with an editor; I don't know
what her reason was, or maybe she always dressed somewhat formally. Her only jewelry was simple gold hoop earrings. I'm not suggesting she was a double, or anything the
least bit surreal, nor am I recounting a dream with subtle
psychological undertones. We all know those irritating story endings when the narrator announces it was all a dream,
bringing both relief and disappointment. No, this was a real
movie theater and real shoes were at stake. But people do
fall into types, and we were the same type. She might even
live in my neighborhood, though I hoped not, since then
I'd have to be wary every time I wore the shoes outside.

She said she was going to the manager's office and I
replied, "Fine. You do that. I'm going to find the women's
room. I'll be back." I guessed correctly that she was too well-
bred to try to stop me going to the women's room or to follow me. She stalked off in her stockinged feet and asked an

usher where she could find the manager. Meanwhile, since I knew this theater well, I took the opportunity to leave by a shadowy side exit and quickly hailed a cab.

I raced up to my apartment and unlocked the door swiftly, as if I were being followed, though this was unlikely. How often movies show people rushing into cabs in hot pursuit, telling the driver, "Follow that taxi!" But this was not a movie, and in any case she wouldn't have had time, after locating the manager and waiting for me to return.

So I had my shoes, and they were not only elegant but comfortable, I found, as I moved around my apartment. This was quite an accomplishment for an ordinary afternoon. Though the movie was a pleasant surprise as well. I looked forward to writing the review that evening, while it was still fresh in my mind. I made a pot of coffee, slipped off my new shoes, and sat down to think the whole thing over.

I admit I felt troubled. I had never stolen anything before except when I was a child and a group of us prowled the aisles of the local convenience store, sneaking candy bars into our open backpacks, while one or two of us distracted the clerk at the counter. But I always felt nervous doing that. This time I hadn't felt nervous at all. I had a definite feeling that I was entitled to those shoes. I needed them to avoid pain, and the pain could be severe. Sometimes when I walked I was so conscious of my hurting feet that I could hardly appreciate the passing scene. That woman, as far as I knew, did not have bad feet. I hoped not, anyway. She hadn't mentioned that. But then she wouldn't have, would she, to a stranger? Maybe she felt as I did, that feet were peculiarly intimate.

All my failed efforts to find suitable shoes had earned me the right to the kind I needed. The fact that they came from someone else's feet was insignificant in comparison.

She could find similar shoes. She evidently knew where to get them. She could get a duplicate pair wherever she'd gotten these.

And then, in a flash of esprit d'escalier, it occurred to me that I might have handled the situation very differently. I might have offered to buy the shoes from her. True, such a request would have struck her as bizarre, but maybe if I'd mentioned my feet and offered whatever sum she asked for, however exorbitant, she might have been persuaded.

Or, come to think of it, when I discovered her shoes under my seat I might have turned around courteously to hand them to her and asked where she'd found them, because I would love to get a pair exactly like them. That wouldn't have sounded so bizarre, and most likely she would have told me. Then my search would be over. I could buy as many pairs of comfortable shoes as I wanted, for when it came to shoes, money was no object.

Why hadn't I done that? It was so much more civilized, so much more consistent with my upbringing and my usual behavior. I was not raised to be a thief or to lie openly and boldly. And because I had the uncanny sense that I knew her, that she was very like me, I assumed she would have responded politely and helpfully about where she bought the shoes.

On the other hand, was all this tormenting of conscience (*agenbite of inwit* as James Joyce memorably calls it) really necessary? It was only a pair of shoes, not money or jewels. They were easily replaceable. And the theft was not committed for sinister purposes, or with any bodily harm. But still . . . I kept wavering.

There was no question of returning the shoes, though. Besides the fact that I didn't know where to find her, I needed those shoes. I deserved them. Like her, like anyone, I was entitled to walk in comfort. Why should she enjoy those shoes, which she didn't need—as far as I knew—while I suffered? No, they were mine now. No longer would I walk in pain.

In the end, I accepted the unflattering truth that I could cope with my wavering conscience more easily than with my bad feet. I would never see that woman again, and soon the whole incident would be forgotten, even when I put on the shoes. Maybe they would turn out to be like the dancer's red shoes in the fairy tale: I would never be able to take them off and would have to keep walking. I accepted that too. I even hoped it might happen.

Fragment Discovered in a Charred Steel Box

(Note to reader: These pages are numbered 15–17 and are clearly part of a longer document whose preceding pages have been lost.)

With the data cited above, not to mention the prevailing conditions known and felt throughout the planet, it is clear beyond a doubt that the human project is drawing to a close. Our Committee, appointed to deal with the coming disaster, has pondered long and hard on how best to proceed. From the start of our deliberations it was generally accepted that rather than wait passively for the end, whether its immediate cause is fire or flood, disease or mass social pathology, our best option is to follow an efficient and humane plan for the time remaining. Even the few optimists still among us realize that their efforts simply waste what meager resources we have left.

To begin with, common sense and compassion suggest that children, in particular, need not be subjected to what is sure to be a painful end, with extremes of intolerable weather, typhoons, flooding, famine, and the resulting chaos, as well as disasters as yet unforeseeable. The Committee has therefore agreed that removal of the children will be the most charitable course of action.

It was decided that nine would be the best age for this removal, naturally in the most benign and unthreatening way possible: various drugs have been suggested, and we will leave to doctors the details of administering them. Nine: by that age their parents would have enjoyed the best of their youth, the years of growth and discovery. Nine: before their natures incline towards adulthood and take on the aggression, greed, shortsightedness, and wastefulness that have brought us to our present pass. (Although some precocious children manage to acquire these traits even earlier.)

Previous sections of this document have itemized the financial practices (favoring gross inequities) and aggressive international policies responsible for our nearly unlivable conditions. Most significant, however, is the improvident use of resources leading to the ruin of the natural environment. Likewise, our research has found ample proof from historical data that our species is incorrigible, despite the efforts of countless utopian social programs and humanitarian agencies. The concentration of power and money has poisoned social as well as familial relations, once the most sacred of bonds.

The financial world is in turmoil as never before, exceeding the crises of the Great Depression and the crash of 2008. Multinational banking establishments are unraveling, with clamorous shareholders demanding the return of investments. Agribusiness no longer seeks exorbitant profits but rather is attempting to dispose of excess produce, much of it rotting but nonetheless demanded by the hungry. The Committee has encouraged the wealthy to share their assets with those in need, since bequeathing them to heirs has become meaningless. Creditors are in retreat, given the futility of pressuring debtors whose only goal is securing food and shelter.

The ironies are not lost on us. Had these measures been adopted sooner, we might have averted what lies ahead.

But unfortunately, only the certainty of the coming end has brought about what the best efforts at amelioration failed to produce.

No amount of investment in technology has managed to stem the proliferation of war, which has contributed to social anomie, refugee camps, and an increasing number of atrocities. The spate of mass murders that began some years ago has grown uncontrollably. It is also worth noting that the suicide rate among people over fifty has risen exponentially, leaving the funeral and cemetery businesses overwhelmed. Volunteers are already being sought to help with rituals and disposal.

Police vigilance and harshness are constant, and the prison population continues to grow. The Committee has done its utmost to avoid a police state; nevertheless, certain measures (outlined above) restricting civil liberties have been unavoidable.

Sterilization clinics are being set up globally, in every large city and in selected rural locations. These will not be administered by force—at least not in our country, which has always prided itself on its democratic principles. In any case no coercion should be needed; most people will probably seek them out willingly. Only a few, probably teenagers or young adults without the benefit of experience, will choose to bear children despite the very brief and harsh lifespans those children can expect.

Those same teenagers and young adults are crucial to the Committee's plans, especially the most hardy and ingenious among them. They will be needed to outline and manage the ultimate details, namely, distribution of drugs and supervision of their use, and formation of armed bands to protect the weak, the disabled, and the elderly from predators.

Among the shrinking number of industries only travel thrives: those who are still able-bodied wish to explore the natural beauties and renowned artifacts of the doomed planet, despite the discomforts caused by scarcity. Travel is more affordable than before, since in our largely ad hoc modes of survival, money has lost much of its value and border controls, in the general chaos, are no longer stringent.

We plan to place many copies of this document (in every major language) in fireproof containers along with other materials pertaining to our history—its glories along with its failures. Scientists will determine where best to deposit them. It may be unreasonable to hope that they can survive, and even more so to hope that a future civilization, if one evolves, will be able to decode them. But this is our only chance to say, simply, that we have been here.

Castles in the Air

The prolific writer, the writer blessed with the famously fertile imagination, was now advanced in age and hadn't an idea in his head. This had never happened to him before. Since his late twenties, he'd written book after book, most of them well received, a handful not. He was not deterred by adverse criticism; he just kept going and expected he would never stop. This emptiness, blankness, was entirely new, and he suffered from it.

It was probably due to his illness; he was aware of that. But just because his organs were betraying him, must his mind betray him too? Or maybe it wasn't the illness but the drugs he was given that hollowed out his imagination. He stopped taking them for a few days, but that didn't work; the pain was too great. Instead he willed himself to keep his mind clear, as if he could control the circulation of his drug-laden blood and bar the chemicals from reaching his brain.

His body continued to wither away. He had no more desires or longings except the one fervent longing for a story. He didn't care to eat much, but his imagination needed to be fed. It howled with starvation, like a neglected infant. This hunger for a story he could get lost in, as he had been lost in stories all his life, was a malady worse than the one gouging out his body.

He slept at odd hours, mostly during the day. At night

he lay awake waiting for images, for the tiniest snatches of something he could latch on to. And then, one night, it was like a miracle, something did come. It was small, a moth of an idea, but it moved towards the light. It grew, carrying with it the seed of a story, happenings, characters, a metaphorical structure. As it grew, he thought it might be the best idea he had ever had. It would make a magnificent book. He could see it rising before him like a great architectural structure, as if he were drawing it in the air in front of him with a magical pen, like the structures computers could generate out of simple lines and curves. But this one was better. It was not programmed or mechanical; it was unique. Towers and turrets appeared in midair, with gleaming mullioned windows, not quite a palace, not quite a cathedral, something entirely original and never before envisioned. It abounded in curves and angles, a complex pattern that appeared random but nonetheless concealed signs of form and intention, repetitions and variations as in a symphony. A visual symphony with interlacing themes.

He was entranced by what his imagination was building and glimpsed how it might translate into words, sentences, paragraphs. If only he could hold a pen long enough to complete it; he was too weak to sit in front of a screen and type the words.

He started to elaborate passages in his mind, bits of description and narrative, characters exchanging speech, when he felt a sudden weakness assail him, a weakness worse than what he had been feeling all these months, as if all the fluid were being drained from his body. He closed his eyes. Behind his lids he kept seeing the structure, multicolored and shimmering, brilliant in the darkness. His breathing became labored; each breath was a tremendous effort but he must keep going for as long as it took. He wrote wildly in his head, words sliding forth, details coming into focus...

Finally, after one agonizing breath, he could breathe no more. But he had it. He had it all. He felt it living inside him the way a woman, he imagined, must feel carrying an unborn child. Unlike a child, it would evaporate with him, but he no longer cared about its tangible existence. This, the conception and gestation, was all that mattered. With his last exhalation, he was satisfied, his hunger appeased. His final sensation was gratitude.

The Page Turner

The page turner appears from the wings and walks on-stage, into the light, a few seconds after the pianist and the cellist, just as the welcoming applause begins to wane. By her precise timing the page turner acknowledges, not so much humbly as serenely, lucidly, that the applause is not meant for her; she has no intention of appropriating any part of the welcome. She is onstage merely to serve a purpose, a worthy purpose even if a bit absurd—a concession, amid the coming glories, to the limitations of matter and of spirit. Precision of timing, it goes without saying, is the most important attribute of a page turner. Also important is unobtrusiveness.

But strive though she may to be unobtrusive, to dim or diminish her radiance in ways known only to herself, the page turner cannot render herself invisible, and so her sudden appearance onstage is as exciting as the appearance of the musicians; it gives the audience an unanticipated stab of pleasure. The page turner is golden-tressed—yes, "tresses" is the word for the mass of hair rippling down her back, hair that emits light like a shower of fine sparkles diffusing into the glow of the stage lights. She is young and tall, younger and taller than either of the musicians, who are squarish, unprepossessing middle-aged men. She wears black, a suitable choice for one who should be unobtrusive. Yet the arresting manner in which her black clothes shelter her flesh, flesh that seems molded like clay and yields to the fabric with a certain playful, even droll resistance, defies unobtrusiveness. Her black long-sleeved knit shirt reaches just below her waist, and the fabric of her perfectly fitting black slacks stirs gently around her narrow hips and thighs. Beyond the hem of her slacks can be glimpsed her shiny, but not too conspicuously shiny, black boots with a thick two-inch heel. Her face is heart-shaped, like the illustrations of princesses in fairy tales. The skin of her face and neck and hands, the only visible skin, is pale, an off-white like heavy cream or the best butter. Her lips are painted magenta.

Of course she is not a princess or even a professional beauty hired to enhance the décor but most likely, offstage, a music student, selected as a reward for achievement or for having demonstrated an ability to sit still and turn the pages at the proper moment. Or else she has volunteered for any number of practical reasons: to help pay for her studies, to gain experience of being onstage. Perhaps she should have been disqualified because of her appearance, which might distract from the music. But given the principles of fair play and equal opportunity, beauty can no more disqualify than plainness. For the moment, though, life offstage and whatever the page turner's place in it might be are far removed from the audience, transported as they are by the hair combed back from her high forehead and cascading in a loose, lacy mass that covers her back like a cloak.

In the waiting hush, the page turner lowers her body onto a chair to the left and slightly behind the pianist's seat, the fabric of her slacks adjusting around her recalcitrant hips, the hem rising a trifle to reveal more of her boots. She folds her white hands patiently in her lap like lilies resting on the surface of a dark pond and fixes her eyes on the sheets of music on the rack, her body calm but alert for the moment when she must perform her task.

After the musicians' usual tics and fussing, the pianist's last-minute swipes at face and hair, the cellist's slow and fastidious tuning of his instrument, his nervous flicking of his jacket away from his body as if to let his torso breathe, the music begins. The page turner, utterly still, waits. Very soon, she rises soundlessly and leans forward—and at this instant, with the right side of her upper body leaning over the pianist, the audience inevitably imagines him, feels him, inhaling the fragrance of her breast and arm, of her cascading hair; they imagine she exudes a delicate scent, lightly alluring but not so alluring as to distract the pianist, not more alluring than the music he plays.

She stays poised briefly in that leaning position until with a swift movement, almost a surprise yet unsurprising, she reaches her hand over to the right-hand page. The upper corner of the page is already turned down, suggesting that the page turner has prepared the music in advance, has, in her patient, able manner (more like a lady-in-waiting, really, than an idle fairy-tale princess), folded down all the necessary corners so that she need not fumble when the moment arrives. At the pianist's barely perceptible nod, she propels the page in the blink of an eye through the small leftward arc and smooths it flat, then seats herself, her body drifting lightly yet firmly, purposefully, down to the chair. Once again the edge of her short shirt sinks into her waist and the folds of her slacks reassemble beguilingly over her hips; the hem of her slacks rises to reveal more of her shiny boots. With her back straight, her seated body making a slender black L-shape, once again she waits with hands folded, and very soon rises, quite silently, to perform the same set of movements. Soon this becomes a ritual, expected and hypnotic, changeless and evocative.

The page turner listens attentively but appears, fittingly, unmoved by the music itself; her body is focused entirely on her task, which is a demanding one, not simply turning the pages at the proper moments but dimming her presence, suppressing everything of herself except her attentiveness. But as able as she proves to be at turning pages—never a split second late, never fumbling with the corners or making an excessive gesture—she cannot, in her helpless radiance, keep from absorbing all the visual energy in the concert hall. The performance taking place in the hall is a gift to the ear, and while all ears are fully occupied, satiated—the musicians being excellent, more than excellent, capable of seraphic sounds—the listeners' eyes are idle. The musicians are only moderately interesting to look at. The eyes crave occupation too. Offered a pleasure to match that of the ears, naturally the eyes accept the offering. They fix on the page turner—pale skin, black clothes, and gold tresses—who surely knows she is being watched, who cannot deflect the gaze of the audience, only absorb it into the deep well of her stillness, her own intent yet detached absorption in the music.

The very banality of her task lends her a dignity, adds a richness to her already rich presence, since it illustrates a crucial truth: banality is necessary in the making of splendid music, or splendid anything for that matter, much like the pianist's probable clipping of his fingernails or the cellist's dusting of his bow, though such banalities are performed in private, which is just as well.

And then little by little, while the listeners' eyes yearn towards the page turner, it comes to appear that her purpose is not so banal after all nor is she anything so common as a distraction. Instead it appears that she has an unusual and intimate connection with the music. She is not a phys-

ical expression of it, a living symbol; that would be too fac-
ile. More subtly, she might be an emanation of the music, a
phantom conjured into being by the sounds, but her physical reality—her stylish clothes and shiny boots—contra-
dicts this possibility, and besides, the audience has seen her
enter minutes before the music began and can attest to her
independent life. No, the connection must be this: though
the pianist is clearly striking the keys and the cellist drawing
the bow over the strings (with, incidentally, many unfortu-
nate contortions of his face), it comes to seem, through the
force of the audience's gaze, that the music is issuing from
the page turner, effortlessly, or through some supernatural,
indescribable effort, as she sits in her golden radiance and
stillness. So that as the concert proceeds, the audience gazes
ever more raptly at the page turner. By virtue of her beauty
and their gaze, she has become an ineffable instrument—no
longer a distraction but rather the very source of the music.

Though the concert is long, very long, the air in the hall
remains charged with vitality, the seraphic sounds yielding
an ecstasy for which the entranced listeners silently bless
the page turner. But perhaps because the concert is long
and the page turner is only human, not even a princess, she
cannot maintain her aloof pose forever. Though not flag-
ging in her task, without any loss of efficiency, she begins
to show her pleasure in the music as any ordinary person
might: her eyelids tremble at a finely executed turn, her lips
hint at a smile for a satisfying chord resolution. Her breathing is visible, her upper body rising and sinking with the
undulations of the sounds swirling about her. She leans into
the music, once or twice even swaying her body a bit. While
undeniably pretty to watch, this relaxation of discipline is a
sad portent. It suggests the concert has gone on almost long
enough, that beauty cannot be endlessly sustained, and that

we, too, cannot remain absorbed indefinitely in radiant stillness. We have our limits, even for ecstasy. Banality beckons us back to its leaden, relieving embrace. The ordinary, appreciative movements of the page turner are a signal that the concert will soon end. We feel an anticipatory nostalgia for the notes we are hearing, even for the notes we have not yet heard, have yet to hear, which will be the closing notes. The early notes of a concert lead us into a safe and luxuriant green meadow of sound, a kind of Eden of the ear, but there comes a point, the climax in the music's arc, when we grasp that the notes are curving back and leading us out of the meadow, back into silent and harsher weather.

And this impression of being led regrettably back to dailiness grows still stronger when now and then the pianist glances over at the page turner with a half-smile, a tacit acknowledgment related to some passage in the music, maybe a little problem of page-turning successfully overcome, a private performance within the public performance, which will remain forever unfathomed by the audience and for those instants makes us feel excluded. With their work almost over, the performers can afford such small indulgences—a foretaste of the inevitable melancholy moment when audience and performers, alike excluded, will file out into their lives, stripped of this glory, relieved of its burden.

When the music ends, as it must, the page turner remains composed and still: unlike the musicians, she does not relax into triumphant relief. As they take their bows, they show intimate glimpses of themselves in the ardor of achievement, as well as a happy camaraderie—their arms around each other's shoulders—in which the page turner cannot share, just as she cannot share in the applause or show intimate glimpses of herself. She stands patiently beside her chair near the piano and then, with the same precise timing as at the start, leaves the stage a few seconds after the musicians, deftly gathering up the music from the rack to carry off with her, tidying up like a good lady-in-waiting.

The musicians reappear for more bows. The page turner does not reappear. Her service is completed. We understand her absence yet we miss her, as though an essential part of the lingering pleasure is being withheld, as though the essential instrument through which the music reached us has vanished along with the sounds themselves. We do not wish to think of what ordinary gestures she might now be performing off in the wings, putting the music away or lifting her hair off her neck with long-staved-off weariness, released from the burden of being looked at. We cannot deny her her life, her future, yet we wish her to be only as she was onstage, in the beginning. We will forget how the musicians looked, but ever after when we revisit the music we will see the page turner—black clothes, golden hair, regal carriage—radiant and still, emitting the sounds that too briefly enraptured us.

Acknowledgments

"Truthtelling" appeared in *Speak* and was nominated for a Pushcart Prize award.

"I Want My Car," "Return of the Frenchman," "The Middle Child," parts of "Public Transit," "Breaking Up," "A Few Days Off," and "A Lapse of Memory" appeared in *Agni*.

"The Golden Rule" appeared in *Fifth Wednesday* and was selected for *The O. Henry Prize Stories 2015*.

"The Strong One" appeared in *Fifth Wednesday*.

"Grief" appeared in *Salamander*.

"A Taste of Dust" appeared in *Ninth Letter* and was selected for *The Best American Short Stories 2005*.

"Am I a Thief?" appeared in *Ploughshares*.

"But I Digress..." appeared in *Narrative*.

"Near November" was published in *110 Stories: New York Writes After September 11* (NYU Press).

"The Page Turner" appeared in *The Threepenny Review*, was selected for *The Best American Essays 1998,* and was published in *Face to Face* (Beacon Press).

About the Author

Lynne Sharon Schwartz is the author of twenty-seven books, which include the novels *Disturbances in the Field*; *Leaving Brooklyn*, a finalist for the PEN/Faulkner Award; and *Rough Strife*, a finalist for the National Book Award and the PEN/Hemingway First Novel Award. She has also published essays, short stories, memoirs, poetry criticism, and translations. Schwartz is the recipient of fellowships from the Guggenheim Foundation, the National Endowment for the Arts (in fiction and translation), and the New York State Foundation for the Arts. She has taught widely in the United States and abroad, and currently teaches at the Bennington College Writing Seminars. She is co-founder of Calliope Author Readings, which produces recordings of great American authors reading from their works.